Puffin Books

ANIMAL STORIES

Here is a delightful collection of seventeen true stories about all sorts of unforgettable animal characters. They range from a humble hedgehog and a wounded seagull to the more awesome lion and elephant, but every one of them has some outstanding quality of personality or intelligence to make it memorable.

It's impossible to pick a top favourite from all these remarkable animals. Horse-lovers may vote for Billy, the 'Little Military Learned Horse' that laid the table and made the tea in the circus ring for Philip Astley, and even rode sitting up with him in his carriage, or Morocco, the sixteenth-century wonderhorse who saved his master's life, but others will prefer Shep, the collie who really did understand every word his master said, gentle Lizzie the elephant, or even the author's own wicked pet, Jacka the crow.

The author's affection and true respect for her animal characters shine out from the pages to make this a happy as well as an interesting book, and one that will interest grown-ups as well as children.

Ruth Manning-Sanders

ANIMAL STORIES

Illustrated by Annette Macarthur-Onslow

PUFFIN BOOKS
in association with
Oxford University Press

Puffin Books, Penguin Books Ltd, Harmondsworth, Middlesex, England
Viking Penguin Inc., 40 West 23rd Street, New York, New York 10010, U.S.A.
Penguin Books Australia Ltd, Ringwood, Victoria, Australia
Penguin Books Canada Ltd, 2801 John Street, Markham, Ontario, Canada L3R 1B4
Penguin Books (N.Z.) Ltd, 182–190 Wairau Road, Auckland 10, New Zealand

First published by Oxford University Press 1961
Published in Puffin Books 1980
Reprinted 1985

Set, printed and bound in Great Britain by
Cox & Wyman Ltd, Reading
Set in Monotype Baskerville

Author's Note

This is a book of true stories. Everything in it has really happened, either to animals I know, or to animals written about by other people.

I wish to thank the following publishers, editors, and agents for permission to re-tell some of the stories:

Messrs. Rupert Hart-Davis for the story of 'Ma Shwe' from *Elephant Bill*.

Messrs. Robert Hale for 'The Story of Nyanya' from *My Friend the Chimpanzee* by J. Oberjohann.

Messrs. Burns & Oates for 'Boney, Molly and Waddy' from *Grey Titan* by George Lockhart.

The Editor of the *Wide World Magazine* for 'The Lion in the Sewer' by F. C. Bostock.

Messrs. Curtis Brown for 'Bostock's Lizzie' from *Menageries, Circuses and Theatres* by E. H. Bostock.

Astley's Little Military Learned Horse, Billy, is a well-known character in circus history, and Banks' Morocco is the most famous of all pre-circus performing horses. The exploits of the clever fox and of Bobo, the baboon, will be found in Wood's *Natural History*; and the rest of the stories are about animals I have myself known.

Contents

1. *Mother Bruma*

Where a road wound through a valley, high up in the
Rocky Mountains, Bruma, the black bear, stood at
the roadside and watched the cars go by. Her two
little cubs, Tig and Mig, were peeping at the cars from
behind the trees on the verge.

Mother Bruma was in a very bad temper. Tig and
Mig understood that well enough; she had just given
them each a sound cuffing, for no reason at all that the
cubs could see. They didn't think they had done

9

anything to vex her; they had been good as gold all the morning.

And, in fact, Mother Bruma's bad temper had nothing to do with *them*; but it was a very bad temper, all the same. It was the cars that were vexing her, because they went driving by, one after the other, and scarcely slowed down when they came abreast of her. Of course the people in the cars *looked* at her – who wouldn't look at a handsome black bear standing at the side of the road? But they looked, and drove on, and never stopped. Or if, occasionally, a car did just stop, no sooner did she make a move towards it, than it rushed away at top speed.

It wasn't at all what Mother Bruma expected. It was something new. All her life, up to now, the people had stopped their cars at the sight of her, and opened a window. Then Mother Bruma would amble over to the car window and stand on her hind legs, and the people would rummage in their picnic baskets, and hand out sandwiches and fruit and cakes to her. That, according to Mother Bruma's thinking, was what people were for. If they weren't bringing food for bears, what were they doing driving along the road?

Mother Bruma hadn't much respect for people; but she hadn't any fear of them, either. For up in that part of the Rockies where she lived, all animals were protected. Naturally, they were free to kill each other, and sometimes they did (especially when the terrible grey grizzlies came down from their high mountain lairs in search of food); but no human being was allowed to hunt, or to shoot, or to kill in that area. And even the grizzlies didn't interfere with Mother Bruma. So she wandered where she would, and had an easy life of it, and hadn't even to bother about looking for food, being kept fat by the tourists, who lavished their sandwiches and cakes on her.

Then why, in these last few days, had everything suddenly changed?

Another car coming! If Mother Bruma could have understood what the two people in the car were saying to each other, she would have known the reason for that unwelcome change.

'Oh look, Bill, there's a bear – do stop!'

'No, no, Mabel. Didn't you read the notices?'

'Of course I read them! But what does it matter?'

'It matters a lot. I don't want *you* being mauled!'

'Fiddlesticks! It wouldn't maul anybody, it's perfectly sweet!'

'All the same, we're not stopping.'

And this car, as all the others had done, drove on.

Poor Mother Bruma, what those two people had been saying was all double Dutch to her. *She* hadn't read the notices! She had watched the men putting them up, as she watched everything that went on. But men like these were always doing something on the road, dragging fallen trees on to the verge, or hammering at the road with noisy machines, or filling up pot-holes. And since they weren't good for anything, except an occasional apple-core or cigarette end, Mother Bruma didn't think much of them.

And as to those square bits of white board with big black letters on them, which the men had stuck up on posts for their own amusement – how could Mother Bruma possibly know that it was those very bits of board that had so suddenly changed all the habits of her easy-going life?

IN YOUR OWN INTEREST YOU ARE REQUESTED
NOT TO FEED THE BEARS. ADULT BEARS CAN BE
DANGEROUS. YOU HAVE BEEN WARNED.

The notices were put up because people *had* been mauled. The bears were amiable enough as long as the food lasted; but, when the people in the cars had no more to offer them, they sometimes got angry. And an angry bear, standing on its hind legs, with its long-taloned forepaws and its great head thrust through a car window, is no joke! You may get clawed and bitten and badly hurt before you can drive away.

It really was bad luck for Mother Bruma, having to share in the evil reputation of some of her rougher neighbours! *She* had never mauled anyone in her life; she was exceptionally good-tempered. But that morning, even she was angry, and would have liked to maul somebody – yes, that she would! But nobody gave her the chance. A car would slow down, and the people in it would peer at her; but, before she had time to amble over to them, they sped on their way.

Oh those sandwiches, oh those apples and oranges, oh those sweet cakes! Mother Bruma's mouth watered. Was she never going to taste them again? And what were she and Tig and Mig going to eat now? She didn't want to go grubbing for roots, and tearing bark with her teeth to get at bees' nests; she wasn't used to the hard way of life. Of course, she could go to the hotel by the lake, and turn over their rubbish dump. There were tins on the dump, and they most often had interesting stuff at the bottom of them, some of it white and sweet and sticky, and some of it pink and juicy and sharp-tasting on the tongue. She often took the cubs to the dump in the evening. But that was only like giving a good child a lollipop, or having one yourself; it didn't fill a body up.

Another car coming! A big one with glass sides and twenty or thirty people sitting high up in it! This kind of car was the very best for sandwiches! Surely it would stop? No, it didn't stop. Mother Bruma watched it speed away, and growled sullenly.

Tig and Mig were having a boxing match behind a tree. They stood on their hind legs and whanged away at each other, growling and squealing. Then Tig rolled Mig over, and pounced on her little, light-coloured belly.

'*Wurra, wurra, wurra!* I've killed you now, Mig!'

'Oh no, you haven't!' Mig bounced up on to her feet again. Paws waving, she advanced on Tig. 'I'll kill *you* now – see if I don't.'

Tig dodged round the tree. Then he caught sight of his mother's glossy, thick-furred back. With a spring, he was on her, 'Kill *you* now, Mother Bruma, kill *you* now!' he growled, dragging at her haunches with his small, sharp teeth.

Mother Bruma's ears went flat. She swung round and gave him a cuff on the side of his head that sent him flying. He found himself sitting down behind the tree, howling shrilly. Mig wandered over to him, nosing and sniffing sympathetically.

'Never mind, Tig! Poor Tig, ne-ver mind!' She gave him a pat with her clumsy little paw. 'Come and play!'

Next minute Tig forgot that Mother Bruma had hurt him. He was up on his hind legs again, boxing with his sister.

Mother Bruma turned her head and watched them. Her heart melted: she didn't feel angry any more. What a handsome little boy and girl she had! Weren't they just lovely? Those people in the cars were missing something! If they would only stop and be nice to her, she would bring Tig and Mig over to show to them. That would be something they'd never forget! Only a few days ago, before the cars had taken to this new stupid habit of rushing by, a woman had got out of a car, and picked Mig up in one arm, and Tig in the other, and kissed their little round heads, and exclaimed, 'Oh, the darlings! Aren't they just *perfect*!' (That was right, they were perfect.) And the man with her had said, 'Stay like that half a sec, and I'll snap you.'

Then the man had taken out a little box, and put it to his eye; and though Mother Bruma didn't know exactly what he was doing, she had understood that it was all part of the admiration. After that, she and the cubs had had strawberries, and she had drunk something sweet and hot out of a cup, holding the cup in her claws. And she had thrown away the cup when it was empty, and that had made the man and woman laugh. She enjoyed making people laugh – when she felt like laughing herself.

'Oh, the darlings! Aren't they just *perfect*!' Mother Bruma looked proudly at her offspring. Suddenly she had an idea. She pounced on Tig, picked him up by the scruff of his neck, and carried him, meekly dangling, out from behind the tree.

'And don't you dare move!' she said, dumping him down in the very middle of the road.

Then she fetched Mig, and dumped her down beside Tig.

'Stay where you are!' she said sharply, and herself went to hide amongst the trees, and watch.

Tig and Mig sat very still. They were like two little wooden images, sitting there in the road. When

Mother Bruma spoke like that, they knew what to expect if they disobeyed.

A car coming! A car that would *have* to stop! It couldn't run over Tig and Mig. And, when it did stop, it would be, 'Oh, the darlings!' and out would come the sandwiches and the cakes. Nobody could resist those two!

Yes, Mother Bruma was right. The car slowed down, it crawled, it stopped. And, out from the back, scrambled four excited children.

'Look, Mum! Look, Dad! Oh, aren't they *sweet*! Can we pick them up? Can we feed them? What do they eat? Sugar? Cake? Quick, where's the hamper?'

Mum and Dad were out of the car too, now. Tig was being cuddled in one child's arms, Mig in another's.

'Gently, children! Don't smother them!'

But Tig and Mig liked being smothered. They didn't care how boisterously they were handled, provided there was food going. Mig's little nose was plastered with cream cake. Tig had a banana in his claws.

'Mum, Mum! Look how he's eating it! Just like a tiny little man!'

Out from behind the trees, Mother Bruma came sauntering. She was all smiles inside herself. But she hadn't a very expressive face. The children shrank back a little, and put the cubs down in the road.

'Mum, is she angry with us? Oh Dad, *don't* let her be angry!'

'No, I'm sure she's not angry. She wants some food too, of course.'

Timidly a child offered Mother Bruma a large slice of cake. Mother Bruma snapped it up. She lolled out a red tongue, and licked her muzzle. Then she performed what she understood to be her most alluring trick. A trick that had never yet failed. She stood erect, swayed her body from one heavy hind foot to another, and waved her arms.

'She's dancing, she's dancing!' The children were in ecstasies. Recklessly they turned out all the contents of the food hamper; and Mother Bruma caught all they tossed her in her big claws, whilst Tig and Mig sat in the road and stuffed themselves.

'There's not going to be much left for us,' laughed the mother.

'Oh, what does it matter?' cried the children.

'Looks as if we'll have to get *our* lunch at the hotel,' said the father.

They gave Mother Bruma a box of chocolates, and she crunched the lot. They gave her a bottle of milk, and she sat on her haunches, took the bottle between her claws, threw back her head, tipped the bottle over her mouth, and emptied it in a series of continuous swallows.

'Oh, clever mother bear! Isn't she *cute*?' cried the children.

But they didn't know just how cute. When there was nothing left to eat, and the family had driven away with the children waving from the windows, the cubs were gorged, and Mother Bruma's stomach was feeling full and contented; and, what was far more important, her mind was at rest. The notices might say what they liked: no car was going to rush by if Mother Bruma wanted it to stop. And she and Tig and Mig were sure of their daily bread for the whole of the summer.

2. *The Fox*

'See that old tree, t'other side of the long fence? Well, I'll tell you a story about that tree; but you must promise me first that you'll never repeat it to a living soul. You do promise? All right, here goes!

'First, as to fox-hunting. I never did hold with it. Foxes are dratted nuisances, I'll own; and if one came-a-prowling after my ducks, I'd up with my gun, and shoot it dead. But that's different from a-chasing of the poor beast up hill and down dale for hours and hours, and letting it be torn to pieces in the end afore your very eyes – and enjoying the sight of it, too! A lady that enjoyed her sport, once went so far as to tell me that the *fox* enjoyed it as much as she – did you ever? How would *she* enjoy being chased over hill and dale, and torn to pieces by a pack of dogs, I'd like to know?

'Well, those are my private feelings. And if you ask what have my private feelings to do with the story, I'll tell you. It's because I feel as I do, that you've given me your solemn word to tell no one what I'm going to tell *you*. For you see, my story is really about a fox.

'This fox is about the wiliest creature that ever trod the earth, I should think, and that's saying a deal. Now, you look at that field, a minute. It's big and it's briary, isn't it? And the briars grow thick and high against the far fence, don't they? And beyond the fence there's that old tree, isn't there? And it's standing a goodish bit back from the fence, mind you. And behind the old tree there's a big wood. All right? Now you take all that well in your eye, whilst I go on with the tale.

'They've been hunting this here fox for years. He's a big 'un, and his coat's got a more than ordinary amount of black in it, and that's how you can tell it's himself. I can't say where his earth is, exactly, but it's somewhere in this neighbourhood; and whenever the huntsmen are out with the hounds and start this here fox, sooner or later you'll see him coming across that briary field. Aye, I've seen him many's the time, and most often not particularly hurrying himself, neither, though the hounds are on his track and baying murder.

'Well, it's always the same tale. He gets to the far side of the field, amongst the briars by the fence, and then he clean disappears, and there's no scent nor sight of him from that moment. The hounds run up and down by the fence, baying and howling and sniffing, and hold up their paws, the way they have; till they get that discouraged they come creeping back with their tails down. But they never find that wily old fox; and I dare swear they never will.

'Aye, I expect that old fox has had many a chuckle to himself over the way he fools them. And he'd chuckle the more if he could hear some of the tales that's going about. Some do say he ain't not a true fox at all, but the devil that's taken a fox's shape for his own amusement. And some do go so far as to say he must be able to fly, or make himself invisible when he's so minded. Fox-hunters from other parts bring their packs across country, miles and miles, to have a run at him; but they all go home properly flummoxed, same as our locals. And may they ever be so, says I! Why, I truly believe that if he was to walk into our farmyard and catch up a duck, I wouldn't have the heart to raise my gun at him. That's the way I've come to think of him – kind of respectful, like.

'There was a gentleman one day as thought he'd solved the mystery.

'"'Tis plain as daylight," says he. "When the fox comes to the fence, he jumps on top of it, and runs along a goodish way to put the hounds off the scent, and then he jumps down on t'other side, and makes for the wood."

'Well, they thought that might be it, and they were for cutting down the fence. But you see, it's *my* fence, and I wasn't having that. So then this gentleman, he has the pack gathered together, and follows the fence round to the end of it, and so jumping a gate and into the wood on t'other side.

'"Now," says he, when they got into the wood, "we'll pick up the old rascal's scent again in no time."

'And did they? No, they didn't. And they went home flummoxed, as usual.

'Now *I* didn't know what become of that fox, no more than anyone else. But somewhere he *must* go. So, thinks I, I'll keep a watch, and find out. So next time the pack was out our way, I went and hid in the woods, and waited.

'By and by I hears the hounds baying across the field.

'Aha! thinks I, they're after him!

'So I parts the branches of a bush I was hid behind, and peers through. And what do I see but the old fox walking along the top of the fence, balancing himself as careful and dainty as if he'd been a rope-dancer. So the gentleman was right, so far. But just you wait a bit!

'I crept out of my hiding-place, and followed along the fence after him, keeping a fair distance back; though I don't expect the old fellow had any thoughts to spare for *me*, with all that pack of dogs after him.

'Some goodish way he walked along the fence top, before the hounds came up on the field side of it, and halted at the place he'd jumped up, and began their racket, running round and hollering. They're getting a real downhearted lot, is that pack, so often they've come across that field, only to be flummoxed! Well, when the fox hears them under the fence at the place he'd jumped up, he stops and turns his head and looks back, disdainful like. So, after he's had a good look back, on he goes again, hurrying a bit now. But he doesn't go very far. When he comes opposite that old tree, he stops again.

'Now you've got your eye on that old tree, haven't you? It ain't touching the fence in any way, is it? No. Agreed. How far off from the fence is it, then? Twelve feet? More than that, you say? Well, make it sixteen feet. But it ain't growing what you might call straight, exactly, is it? It's leaning a bit to one side; and though it's sprouting branches at the bottom, the top of it's gone dead; for it come to grief in a great storm – aye, I can call it to mind – years and years ago, when I was a nipper. It was a mighty tree in them old days, must have stood a hundred feet, shouldn't wonder, though now not more than thirty. And if you was to look closer, though you can't see it from here, you'd see it has a kind of knot, or hump in its trunk, where it begins to lean to one side. Like an old man bowed a bit with the years.

'So the fox stops opposite this tree. And what does he do next? He stoops himself together, and he takes a high and long bound, and clears that sixteen feet that's between him and the tree, and lands, all four feet tucked up close, on this here hump. Never could have believed it! They as said he could fly weren't so far wrong, after all...

'No, I haven't finished yet. Having landed safe on that hump, he doesn't waste time staying there. Up the trunk he runs till he comes to the top, and then – he disappears! My days! I didn't know it then, but I know it now: *that tree's hollow!*

'Many and many an hour he's stayed safe and sound, tucked up inside that hollow tree, I reckon: till the hunt's called off, and night falls, and he can come out, and make his way home.

'How does he get out? Now that I can't tell you: down to the ground in the wood, I shouldn't wonder. Anyways, I should think it'd be easier getting down than getting up...

'Now you recollect your promise, mind. And don't you never breathe a word to no one of what I've been telling you.'

3. *Sally*

'Elephants are funny,' says Bill. 'You just been having a look at Sally?'

'Yes,' I said. 'And I was surprised not to find you in the tent with her. She was so fond of you, she would scarcely let you out of her sight; and here she is, now, with a new fellow to look after her. And you – what are you doing, grooming the horses?'

Bill scratched his cheek thoughtfully. 'Darned if I know – exactly,' he said. 'But *she* knows. And once she takes a whim into her head, well there you are – elephants are funny. I daren't go near her these days. See my left arm? Can't lift it no higher than my shoulder, nor ever will again. Well, *she* done that.'

'What, *Sally*?' I couldn't believe it!

'Yes, she done it,' repeated Bill. 'And though it hurt me bad enough in the body, I think it hurt me worse in my feelings. You remember, before the war, how she used to be roaming about the field between shows, and how I had only to sing out to her and she would come straight over to me, and twine her trunk round my neck?'

'Yes, I remember. And if ever an elephant loved a man, Sally loved you.'

'Ah,' says Bill, 'but it seems love can turn to hate in elephants, same as in humans.'

'What happened?' I asked.

'It was this way,' says Bill. 'At the beginning of the war I was called up and went overseas; and though I thought of Sally quite often, I never got home to have a glimpse of her all through them years. But when I was demobbed, I wrote to the Boss asking could I have my old job back to look after Sally. And he wired back, "Yes, come at once." So back I came.

'I'd been kept a while in Germany after the fighting stopped. It was the spring of the year before I got home, and the circus had already taken the road. I joined them at Cuckborough, a nice little town, and found them in a fine big field, with trees round it, and daisies lying thick as snow on the grass.

'First thing I see when I come into that field was Sally, roaming amongst the daisies. And *was* I pleased to see her? I'll say I was! I gave her my usual call right across the field, and she cocked up her ears, and listened. Then over she comes, straight to me, in that leisure-like, light-footed way of hers.

'"Well, Sal, old girl!" says I.

'And you may call me soft, but I was that glad to be with her again that tears come into my eyes.

'She stretches out her trunk, same as she's always done. But did she twine it nice and loving round my neck? No, she did not! Believe me, or believe me not, she winds it tight round my body, swings me off my feet, high in the air, and flings me far away from her, like so much dirt. I landed a crack on my arm, and broke it up bad, as you can see. And I came near to breaking my heart, too. And never since that day have I dared go near her, for there's a look in her eye that tells me plain as plain, "You just keep off!"'

'But it's unbelievable!' I said. 'Why did she do it?'

'That's what I've asked myself many's the time,' says Bill. 'And by what I can figure out, it's this way. She missed me bad when I went away – the Boss told me that: wouldn't eat for a long time, and pined and moped, and grew real thin and sickly. She must have

been wondering to herself why I'd left her. *She* couldn't know there was a war on ...

'Aye, her feelings must have been properly hurt to think I'd gone off and deserted her. After him and me had been so chummy together, thinks she. After the way I loved that fellow! He just walks out on me, and leaves me lonesome! Then, when she begins to pick up a bit, she thinks, well, I can live without him, I suppose. There's other fellows in the world beside him, ain't there? And she turns her heart to her new keeper.

'But there's a place in her heart that keeps sore at me; and when she hears my voice again, that sore part blazes up into a flame of anger. "Think you can leave me and come back to me just when and how you please?" says she. "Well, you can't! I've got my pride! So take *that*, you faithless, fickle-hearted fellow!" And whang! Away I'm throwed ...

'And if I live to be a hundred,' says Bill, 'I shan't never be able to explain to her how it all come about. So I've just got to lump it – and that's the reason you find me here, a-grooming of these dratted horses, and not in the place I belong to be at all.'

4. *A Dog in a Million*

'That dog, Shep,' said Farmer Nicholls, 'he mayn't be what you'd call a thoroughbred, exactly – got a bit of this and that in him, I dare say – but he's one in a million. He understands every word I say.'

Shep, the Scotch collie, was lying on the hearth-rug in front of the kitchen fire, with his nose between his paws. One of his eyes was brown, and one blue, which gave his face a strange expression. Hearing himself praised, he raised his head an inch or two, glanced up at his master, and wagged his tail. Then he rolled over on his side, gave a contented sigh, and shut his eyes.

He was going to have a nice, long snooze. He had had a heavy day of it, rounding up the sheep from the hills, and bringing them down and getting the silly things between the hurdles to be dipped. What a fuss they made over it, baaing and kicking! You'd think they were going to be murdered, instead of just being plumped into the sheep-dip and out again.

After the sheep were dipped, he had driven them back to pasture again; and by then it was time to bring in the cows to be milked. But the cows didn't give him any trouble, they were more sensible than the sheep. Some of the heifers were skittish, of course. They liked to put down their heads, and take little sideways runs at him; and to pretend, too, that they had as much right as the cows to go out of the meadows to the milking shed. He had to growl at them a bit, to teach them to keep back. But they did keep back – he wasn't having any nonsense! And it was a great pleasure, after that, to get the milking cows moving in slow and orderly procession through the meadows to the farmyard gate, and through the gate to the milking shed. All his master had to do, was to stand by the gate and open it, and shut it again. Shep could manage all the rest.

Whilst the cows were being milked, Shep had waited, as usual, at the door of the shed, to drive them back into the meadows for the night. That finished his work for the day. He had had a good supper, and now, in the early evening, he could stretch out before the fire, relax, and snooze.

'You'd say he was sleeping now, wouldn't you?' said Farmer Nicholls. 'And so he may be, *kind* of sleeping. But sleeping or waking, it's all one to Shep – *he* don't miss anything! In a minute I'll prove it to you about him understanding every word. He mayn't be paying particular heed just now, because what I'm saying don't concern his duties; it's just babble, babble, like, and a waste of his time to attend to. But when what I'm saying *does* concern his duties, well...!

'Now you and me will just go on with our talk, nice and comfortable, and by and by you'll see. You was asking me about the price of lambs now: well, I can't complain, might be better, might be worse. But the fact is, sir,' (Farmer Nicholls winked at his visitor, and went on talking in exactly the same quiet, even-toned voice), 'the cows are in the corn, and so . . .'

Shep didn't wait to hear any more. In an instant he had leaped to his feet, and was running to the door. The door was shut; he didn't wait for it to be opened – he gave a jump through the open window, and was gone.

'There!' said the farmer proudly. 'What did I tell you? I didn't raise my voice, now, did I? Nor yet break off what I was a-saying of. I was running on in my speech smooth and placid, like a quiet river, as you might say. Yet that dog heard! He won't come back now, till he's been the round of the cornfields. Shame to tease him, but – '

Farmer Nicholls got up, opened the kitchen door, and stood looking out into the twilight. 'Yes, a dog in a million,' he repeated. 'Ah, here he comes!'

Shep came running in. He was panting, and his tongue was hanging out. He'd been very worried for a few minutes; but it was all right – his master had made a mistake. He flumped down on the hearth-rug again.

'Bit hot in here,' said the farmer. 'We'll leave the door open, sir, if it's all the same to you.' He came back to his seat, and went on talking. 'We was speaking of the price of lambs, sir, wasn't we? Well, you see, it's all according to the supply and demand. You have to study your markets, and sell at the right time. But, well, there it is,' (he winked at his visitor again), 'since the cows are in the corn, you don't . . .'

Shep got up and shook himself. Out of his one brown and one blue eye he looked doubtfully at his master. Then he walked to the door, and gazed out into the twilight. Oh well, he supposed he'd have to go and see. But he didn't hurry, this time. Of course, a dog *might* make a mistake, but he really had felt quite sure that the cows were all in the meadows. Could he have overlooked Molly, or Whiteface, or Crumplehorn? Crumplehorn was a jumper, she *might* have leaped the hedge, and where she went, Molly and Whiteface always tried to follow . . .

So through the meadows, and round the cornfields, went Shep once more. But there was nothing to worry about. No cow was in the corn. They were all in the meadows, where they should be: some lying down, and some standing, some tearing at the grass greedily, some leisurely chewing the cud, some blowing out their breath with great snorts, in surprise at seeing him. Not till he had gone the round of every beast in the herd, heifers and all, did Shep return. And then he walked in through the kitchen door with a good deal of dignity, and settled himself with a sigh on the hearth-rug again.

Farmer Nicholls was still talking. He had gone from lambs to horses now, and from horses to tractors.

'Handy things them machines,' he said. 'Can't think how we ever did without 'em.' He winked at his visitor for the third time. 'And if it wasn't for the fact that the cows are in the corn, I'd – '

But this was too much! Shep opened his one brown and his one blue eye, raised his head, and stared at his master. Had the man gone mad? He stared at his master, and – yes, he *growled*! He put his nose between his paws, and growled once more. Not a fierce growl, but a very determined one.

'If you think I'm going out again on a wild goose chase, you're mightily mistaken!' that growl said.

Farmer Nicholls was laughing softly. 'Shame to tease you, ain't it, Shep? Here, let's see if we can find you a marrow bone.' He ambled off into the pantry, and came back with a big, meaty bone. 'That's with my apologies, Shep,' says he. 'Here, shake hands, and say as you've forgiven me.'

Shep stood up, and gave his paw to his master. His expression was very grave. 'I do forgive you, but I don't see that you need have done it, all the same,' he was saying.

'Was just my way of showing you off, Shep,' explained Farmer Nicholls. He turned to his visitor. 'Now you get my meaning, don't you, sir? He's a dog in a million, is Shep.'

'I think you're right,' said the visitor, as he got up to take his leave.

5. *The Lion in the Sewer*

Many years ago, young Frank Bostock brought his menagerie to the three days' Onion Fair in Birmingham. In the menagerie was a lion called Nero. Nero was a beautiful creature, big, sleek, and tawny, with a great, chubby head and strong shoulders, covered with a handsome dark mane. A real king of beasts – young Frank Bostock was very proud of him.

Well, the menagerie was set up on the fair-ground, with the animal cages arranged on three sides·of an open square, so that people could walk all the way round. And on the fourth side of the square was the show-front, made of cloth that was coloured and gilded, and had huge pictures of animals painted all over it. And, on a platform under the show-front sat eight bandsmen, wearing scarlet tunics and leopard-skin hats, and playing away on their brass instruments to attract the crowds.

Young Frank Bostock walked round his show, examining everything, to make sure that all was in order. All was in order, and he felt well pleased.

'I think, though,' says he, 'we'll shift Nero into a larger cage. He's grown too big for the one he's in.'

So his men brought up another cage, and put a big chunk of meat in it, and opened the doors of both cages, and tried to persuade Nero to go into the new one.

But something frightened Nero; perhaps it was the noise of all the thousands of people who had come to see the fair, though he should have been used to fair-ground noises by this time; or perhaps it was some little thing, like a piece of broken glass, glittering in the sun, that he didn't understand. At any rate, *something* frightened him, and instead of going into the new cage, he made a sudden dash out of the cage he was in; and, before anyone could stop him, he had rushed right out of the menagerie, and into the open fair-ground.

'There's a lion loose! A *lion*! ... There *is*. I tell you! Oh, oh, here he comes! ... Run for your lives! ... Run! Run! Run!'

All those thousands of people on the fair-ground were shouting and screaming and running in all directions!

Poor Nero, more frightened than ever at all the hubbub, tore straight across the fair-ground, and out at the gates, and away through the streets of the city. Men, women, and children fled before him, the women dropping their shopping baskets, the business men losing their hats and their attaché cases in their panic, the shopkeepers slamming and bolting their doors, the policemen running and blowing their whistles, men in carts urging their horses at a gallop down side-streets – the whole city was in the wildest confusion.

The streets behind Nero were crowded with shouting people, but the streets in front of him were emptied as if by magic; and on and on he ran, right through the city, and through the suburbs, and into the country, till he came to a small brook, and into that brook he jumped – and disappeared!

What had happened? Just this. Under the waters of that small brook was a hole that led into the town sewers, and Nero had dropped right through this hole. And here he was now, wandering about underground through the sewer tunnels, that ran for miles and miles beneath the town.

At intervals along these tunnels, were the man-holes, or openings, for workmen to go down and inspect the drains; and, whenever Nero came to one of these man-holes, he let out a loud roar. Very soon an enormous crowd of people had gathered along the brook-side, listening to Nero's progress down below, as he stopped at every man-hole, and sent up deep-chested roar after roar, that echoed along the enclosed space of the sewer tunnels, so that the very earth itself seemed to be roaring, and the listeners grew half wild with terror.

Nero was not really a savage animal. Frank Bostock who, young as he was, was known to be one of the greatest animal trainers then living, could usually do anything with him. He would pat and fondle the great chubby head, tickle the big sleek body (Nero loved to be tickled) and get him to take food out of his hand. But now that Nero was so excited and terrified, young Frank knew that there would be no doing anything with him, and that it would be impossible to entice him out of those sewers.

What on earth was to be done? Every now and then a man would come running to say that Nero's great head had been seen poking up from this man-hole or that, with his eyes glaring, and his ears flat, and his lips lifted in a snarl – people were imagining that they could see him everywhere! And every now and then, a policeman would come up and tell Frank that there were a hundred thousand people on the fair-ground, half mad with fear, and threatening a riot; and that he must, he simply *must*, do something!

So young Frank decided that he *would* do something. If he couldn't catch Nero, he could at least quieten the people by pretending to catch him. So he chose out one or two of his most trusted animal keepers, and told them what he intended to do.

The keepers went back to the menagerie, and put another lion, a very old and quiet one, called Punch, into a shifting den. The den had a partition in it, worked by a spring, and Punch was behind this partition. Then the men covered the den over completely with thick canvas, so that no one could see Punch inside; and after that, they hoisted it up, lion and all, on to a wagon drawn by two horses.

Away went the wagon, rumbling through the city, and out through the suburbs, followed by a huge crowd of excited people. When they reached the brook, the den was taken off the wagon, and placed in front of the man-hole down which Nero had disappeared.

Meanwhile, some distance away, one of the lion trainers, Orenzo, entered the sewer by another man-hole. Orenzo was carrying a strange assortment of weapons with him: a revolver, a bundle of fireworks – such as Roman Candles and crackers – a frying-pan, and a thick stick. And he also took Marco, Frank Bostock's boarhound, with him.

Slowly, slowly, Orenzo and Marco crawled along the sewer in the direction of the brook. Orenzo was making as much noise as he possibly could, setting off his fireworks, banging with the frying-pan, beating the sides of the tunnel with his thick stick, and urging on Marco to bark and growl his loudest.

'Well, certainly,' the waiting crowds told each other, '*something*'s happening down there!' For all this noise was echoing like thunder along the low sewer tunnel, and the thunderous echoes were drawing nearer and nearer to the brook.

Suddenly the noise stopped. There was a moment's complete silence; and then two quick revolver shots. That was the signal young Frank Bostock was waiting for. The men in charge of the shifting den touched the spring, there was a sharp click, the partition fell in, the men snatched the canvas off the den – and there stood a lion, plain for all to see!

It was not Nero of course, it was Punch, but the watching crowd couldn't know that. And sleepy old Punch was playing his part well; for though he had been peacefully snoozing under his canvas covering, the revolver shots had roused him, and he had leaped up with a roar. Now he was actually running to and fro in the shifting den, and lashing his tail – the very image of a ferocious, newly-captured beast!

A great shout went up. 'They've got him! They've got him! They've got the lion!'

In triumphal procession the shifting den was taken back to the menagerie. Orenzo and Marco came up out of the sewer, and Orenzo was carried shoulder-high behind the wagon, amid the cheers of the excited onlookers. That afternoon, over forty thousand people swarmed into the menagerie, and filed past the cage of the mildly surprised old Punch, the supposed fierce lion that had escaped and been captured again. Never had the menagerie done such business! Money was rolling in, but – *Nero was still in the sewer!*

All that night, and all the night after that, young Frank Bostock could not sleep. Having placed armed sentries at the man-hole by the brook, he spent miserable hours of darkness, going round all the other man-holes in the city; watching, listening, but hearing nothing.

He felt simply terrible! And, on Saturday afternoon,

which was the last afternoon of the three days' fair, he went to the Chief Constable, and told him the whole story. At first, the Chief Constable was very angry; but by and by, he calmed down, and said he supposed young Frank had acted for the best. Then together they thought out a plan for the recapture of Nero.

In the small hours of Sunday morning, when all the town was sleeping, two hundred men, policemen and menagerie hands, all sworn to secrecy, assembled in the big menagerie tent. Every man was armed; some with pistols, some with rifles, and some with crowbars, clubs, and carving knives.

Silently the men stole off to their appointed places along the sewers. Every exit was manned, and a shifting den was placed in position at the man-hole down which, three days ago, Nero had disappeared. Then, with three companions, and the boarhound, Marco, young Frank entered the dark and slimy sewer, and began crawling cautiously forward on hands and knees, for there was no room to stand upright.

By and by, Marco gave a sharp bark, followed by a throaty growl; and away in the darkness ahead gleamed two greenish-red eyes. Nero! Young Frank sent one of the men back with the news; and other trainers immediately lowered themselves into other man-holes, to which ropes with slip-knots were also fastened.

Firing off blank cartridges and Roman Candles, Frank and his two companions crawled nearer and nearer to those gleaming eyes, hoping that Nero would turn and retreat to the entrance by which he had come in, and where the shifting den was waiting for him.

But the gleaming eyes did not move: more blank cartridges, a real cascade of Roman Candles, furious growls and barks from Marco. Not a sound, not a movement ahead – the eyes still gleamed in the same place out of the darkness.

Young Frank, deeply puzzled, was considering what next to do, when the valiant Marco lost patience. Bristling and growling furiously, he dashed forward; and there, in that evil-smelling darkness, a ferocious battle raged between dog and lion. Roarings and barkings, growlings, snarlings and howlings, echoed back through the narrow tunnels; the demented Nero lashing out with all his panic strength, the valiant Marco returning again and again to the attack. Only when slashed, bitten, and bleeding from a dozen wounds, and almost at his last gasp, did Marco come crawling back to Frank Bostock for protection. Frank at once told one of his men to take him up to the surface, and have his wounds attended to.

Now there remained in the sewer young Frank and one other man – and ahead of them lurking in darkness, the infuriated Nero. Crouched on hands and knees, with his assistant lying almost alongside, but just a little behind him, all that Frank could see of Nero were those two greenish-red eyes, that glared and gleamed, but never moved.

Why did Nero not move? He *must* be got on the move somehow! The first thing that Frank did was to take off his big jack-boots, and put them on his hands and arms, as a protection against Nero's teeth and claws. Then, inch by inch, he crawled forward.

Still Nero did not move. He just gave a deep, angry growl, that was all. Frank was now so close to him that he could feel Nero's hot breath on his face. If he could but have stood upright, he would have had more chance; but, crouched as he was, his head was at Nero's mercy. If now Nero should lash out with one of his heavy paws, he could split Frank's head open like an egg-shell.

'Quick, the pail! Put the pail over my head,' Frank whispered to his assistant.

This was a large iron pail in which they were carrying their blank cartridges. The man clapped it over Frank's head like a helmet. Frank gave a sudden lurch forward, and brought one of the heavy jack-boots, smack, across Nero's nose.

And still Nero refused to move. He just stopped where he was, growling savagely.

And then, as Frank drew himself together for another smack at Nero, the pail on his head tipped, rolled off, and went clattering down the sewer, making a noise that echoed through the narrow tunnel like clap after clap of thunder. It was too much for Nero, he turned tail – and vanished!

Then they found out why the poor beast had refused to move before. Immediately behind him was an eight-foot fall in the sewer tunnel; and now, somewhere beyond this fall, they could hear him roaring, and roaring, and roaring! Scrambling down the eight-foot drop, they followed the sound, and very soon they found him. In leaping another fall he had caught his hind legs and quarters in one of the slip-nooses that had been lowered from a man-hole. And there he was, hanging upside down, and quite helpless.

Pero Nero! By means of other ropes they speedily managed to turn him right side up. The shifting den was fetched, and set in place above him. And so, wet, cold, covered with filth, and as unlike a king of beasts as anything could well be, they hauled him up, got him into the shifting den, and rushed him back to the menagerie. And there, on a huge bed of straw, with plenty of food and water close beside him, they left him to rest and recover, and clean himself up.

And Marco, the boarhound? Yes, he recovered from his wounds, so all ended happily.

6. *The Story of Nyanya*

I. NYANYA IN AFRICA

Mr Oberjohann was travelling through the forests in Africa, collecting and training young wild animals for the European zoos. For his headquarters he had a big camp, with a lot of keepers and servants. Sometimes they ran short of meat; so one day, Mr Oberjohann took his gun and went off into the forest to see if he could shoot some game.

It was very quiet amongst the great trees of the forest. The trees were intertwined with creepers; and the creepers hung down like thick curtains, shutting him off from all the world. With his gun at the ready, Mr Oberjohann walked on slowly and warily, listening acutely, watching intently, lest some wild beast should spring at him unawares. But he heard nothing, and he saw nothing, till he came to a clearing: and then his heart gave a big jump. For, standing in the middle of the clearing was an enormous gorilla.

Now a gorilla is strong enough to strangle a lion, and an angry gorilla is far more dangerous than any other animal; he will seize you in his great arms, and choke the life out of you without mercy. And the only thing to do, if you would save your life, is to shoot quickly.

But was this gorilla angry?

Mr Oberjohann raised his gun.

'Hoo-ee! Hoo-ee!' said the gorilla.

Mr Oberjohann lowered his gun. He understood. The gorilla wasn't angry; he was friendly; he was saying 'Hullo!'

'Hoo-ee! Hullo!' said Mr Oberjohann.

And what did that gorilla do but come right up to Mr Oberjohann and fling his arms round his neck!

'Well, old fellow,' says Mr Oberjohann, as the gorilla hugged him, 'it's plain to me that you're no *wild* animal. You must belong to someone. Let's see if we can find your master.'

He began to scout round amongst the trees, looking for a track that might lead him to some human dwelling; but he could find none. For a little while the gorilla followed him about, watching curiously. Then he suddenly became impatient, and seized Mr Oberjohann's hand.

'Come on, stupid!' he seemed to be saying. 'This way!'

Pulling Mr Oberjohann behind him, he made his way amongst the trees, pushing aside the thick creepers that barred their progress, and in a very short while they came to a tumbledown hut. Lying on a mat in front of the hut was a man. The man was very old and thin, and he looked ill; but he got up when he saw Mr Oberjohann, bid him good day, and politely offered him a seat on the mat.

They sat down side by side, and the gorilla came and sat close to the old man, who stroked his woolly head, and called him by his name, Nyanya.

'Yes,' said he, 'Nyanya and I are the best of friends. In fact he is the only friend I have. Nyanya, my friend, go and fetch water.'

Nyanya immediately got up and went into the hut. He came out again carrying a water-bottle, and with this he wandered off out of sight.

'Nyanya helps me all he can,' said the old man. 'It is four years since I found him. He was a baby then. His mother had been killed by a poisoned arrow. He was all alone, and I was all alone, so I brought him

41

home with me. I wove baskets, and with the money I earned, I bought milk for him . . . Now you see what a fine, useful fellow he has grown into,' he went on, as Nyanya came back to the hut, carefully carrying the full water-bottle. 'Ah Nyanya, you are indeed my friend, for I have no other!'

Mr Oberjohann felt sorry for the poor old man. He didn't like to leave him all alone in the forest, with no one but a gorilla to look after him. So he offered to take them both back to his camp.

'I have a great many animals in my camp,' he explained. 'I collect them, you know. Would you like to be one of my keepers, and help to look after them? I see you have a way with animals.'

The old man was delighted. He made his few ragged clothes into a bundle, and gave the bundle to Nyanya to carry. Then they all three set out, the old man and the gorilla hand in hand. With his other hand, the old man helped himself along with a stick; whilst, with *his* other hand, Nyanya steadied the bundle which he carried on his back.

Mr Oberjohann noticed a curious thing: Nyanya walked upright; whereas most gorillas, like all the big apes, shuffle along the ground humped up, using the backs of their hands to help their feet.

'Why, Nyanya walks like a man!' he exclaimed.

'How should he not?' said the old man. 'He has seen no one walk but me. And he imitates me in everything.'

When they got to the camp, Mr Oberjohann gave the pair of them a hut to themselves. Nyanya was surprised to see so many people. That evening he wandered about the camp, examining everything; but he was very well behaved, and went to sleep in the hut with the old man, sharing his bed, cuddling up to him, and holding him closely embraced in one great arm.

But, in the morning, long before daylight, Mr Oberjohann was awakened by screams and shouts coming from the kitchen. He jumped out of bed, and ran into the kitchen, and there, by the light of the fire, he saw his cook lying face downward on the floor, with Nyanya standing on the man's back, doing a war-dance, and beating his breast with his fists in time to his dancing.

'Nyanya! Nyanya! *Come here*!' shouted Mr Oberjohann.

But Nyanya was too angry to heed him. He stooped down and began to hammer the cook's head with his fists. The cook was screaming, and the kitchen hands were running about and shouting, 'He'll be killed! He'll be killed!' Nothing Mr Oberjohann could do would stop Nyanya's fury, so he hurried away to call the old man; but in the darkness he couldn't find him.

The screaming and shouting went on. And then, suddenly, there was silence. When Mr Oberjohann got back to the kitchen, he saw Nyanya and the old man coming out of it hand in hand.

The cook was in a bad way, bleeding and moaning. Mr Oberjohann washed his wounds, disinfected them, smeared them with vaseline, and bound them up. Then he went to look for naughty Nyanya.

He found him sitting pressed close up to the old man. He had his arms folded across his chest, and he looked as meek as Moses.

'Nyanya!' said Mr Oberjohann. 'What on earth made you do it?'

'Hoo-hoo!' said Nyanya sadly. 'I'm very sorry, but I couldn't help it.'

The old man explained. It was this way. Ever since

he was a baby, Nyanya had been brought up to do the early morning chores for his master; so he had gone into the kitchen that morning to look for a bucket to fetch water. He found two buckets, and was making off with them, when the cook shouted to him to bring them back. Nyanya walked on. The cook ran after him, and tried to take the buckets from him; but Nyanya wasn't having that. He hung on to his buckets. So then the cook took up a big stick and threatened to beat Nyanya. Nyanya had never been beaten in his life! He flew into a rage.

'What, beat *me*, you impudent little man? Just you dare try!'

The cook thought he would try, so then Nyanya seized him, and flung him face downward, and danced on him. And the more he thought about how he had been insulted, the angrier he became. He really might have killed the cook; but when the old man arrived and called him, he came away like a lamb.

'Nyanya only wanted to make himself useful,' explained the old man. 'Let him do the chores, and you'll see how good he'll be.'

Well, at first the cook wasn't at all willing to have a savage gorilla for a kitchen hand. But Mr Oberjohann talked him round at last; and, from then on, Nyanya drew the water, and brought in the wood, and swept out the kitchen, and fetched and carried, and made himself so useful that very soon he and the cook were great friends.

One day, as Nyanya, having finished his chores to his satisfaction, was looking out of the kitchen door, he saw something that made him stare very hard. There was Mr Oberjohann, without his clothes on, standing in front of a bucket of hot water. But it wasn't the steam from the bucket that made Nyanya stare – he knew all about hot water – it was what Mr Oberjohann was doing. Mr Oberjohann was rubbing his chest, and, as he rubbed, his chest was turning all white and frothy. There was some magic in this! Where was that white froth coming from?

Nyanya stepped away from the kitchen door, and slowly, very slowly and cautiously, circled round Mr Oberjohann, coming all the time a little nearer to him, and still staring open-mouthed. Then he stood still, and began rubbing his hand briskly across his chest, just as Mr Oberjohann was doing.

'Am I getting all white and frothy, am I?' He looked down at his huge chest, and rubbed and rubbed, but nothing happened.

He tried rubbing with both hands, but still nothing happened. It was most disappointing! 'Hoo-hoo!' he said, 'Hoo-hoo! *Why* doesn't the magic work? Why *doesn't* it?'

Then he saw Mr Oberjohann dip his hand into the hot water. Aha! *That* was it! Nyanya dipped *his* hand into the hot water. He kept on dipping and dipping, and rubbing and rubbing; but still his chest wouldn't come white and frothy!

'Here you are, Nyanya,' says Mr Oberjohann. And he held out the cake of soap, which he had kept hidden in his hand.

'Ha!' said Nyanya in triumph, and snatched the soap. 'So *this* is the magic, is it?' First he smelled it carefully, and then he crammed it into his mouth, and swallowed it.

'Now we shall see the magic work!' thinks he, and begins to rub himself harder than ever.

But the magic *won't* work. Moreover, Mr Oberjohann is laughing at him. It's too bad! Look out, Mr

Oberjohann! Nyanya is going to fly into a rage at any moment now. Yes, he *is*!

All wet and soapy as he was, Mr Oberjohann hurried into his tent, brought out another cake of soap, dipped his hand into the hot water, and lathered Nyanya's chest for him. Nyanya's angry looks gave place to a grin of delight. The magic was working at last! Open-mouthed, grinning from ear to ear, he watched his great chest becoming whiter and whiter, and frothier and frothier. Then, shouting with joy, he rushed to the bucket of water, splashed it all over himself, snatched the soap from Mr Oberjohann, and lathered himself from head to foot. *Now* he knew how it was done!

'Ha! Ho!' shouts he. 'Who's the whitest and frothiest of us two now? *I* am! *I* am! And don't you think you're going to make yourself any frothier, because you're not!'

He gives Mr Oberjohann a quick, cunning glance – and swallows what remains of the soap.

Though Nyanya still loved the old man, and every night would go and lie down beside him in his hut, yet he quickly came to realize that in that camp Mr Oberjohann was boss; and so it was Mr Oberjohann that he must now copy in all his ways. Everything that Mr Oberjohann did, *he* must do. He must have his pipe, and smoke it, just as Mr Oberjohann did. And, what was more, when it came to filling the pipes, Nyanya must be handed the tobacco pouch and fill his pipe first, or else Mr Oberjohann might look out for rages. Having seen how the cook was treated, Mr Oberjohann wasn't particularly anxious for rages; and so it soon came about that the real boss in that camp was Nyanya himself.

But when one day Mr Oberjohann was given a box

of cigars, he *did* think he might be allowed to keep them for himself; because cigars in the wilds of Africa were not easy to come by. So he locked the cigars up in a box, all but one; and, when he thought Nyanya wasn't looking, he took this one, and strolled off a little way from the camp to smoke it by himself.

He had just lit up, and was taking his first few puffs, and smiling to himself to think how clever he'd been, when he looked round, and there was Nyanya close behind him!

'Me too!' says Nyanya, holding out his hand.

'No, Nyanya, *no*!' says Mr Oberjohann. 'The cigars are for *me*. If you want a smoke, take some tobacco from my pouch. Here you are!'

He held out the tobacco pouch. Nyanya gave it a scornful look, and walked away with great dignity. 'Oh, all right, if you're so selfish as not to give me that cigar, I shall go and help myself,' thinks he.

And off he goes to get the precious cigar box. But the box was locked! What an insult! Nyanya threw it down, and stalked off to the old man's hut.

For four days after that he didn't come near Mr Oberjohann. And every morning, during those four days, he went off somewhere by himself. What was he up to now? Mr Oberjohann began to feel a bit anxious.

'Does anyone know where Nyanya is?' he asked on the fifth morning.

'Yes, master,' said one of the hands with a big grin. 'Seen him up a mango tree, smoking a cee-gar.'

Mr Oberjohann rushed to his tent. The box of cigars was still locked, and the key was hanging in the usual place. But, when he unlocked the box, he found that several cigars were missing. Nyanya had taken the key, unlocked the box, helped himself, and put the

47

key back where he found it.
The cheek of the creature!
And the cleverness of the
creature! Mr Oberjohann
was so full of admiration
for the cleverness, that he
couldn't feel *very* angry at
the theft.

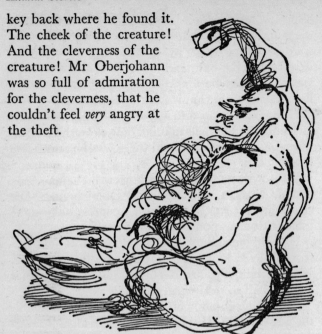

All the same, he wasn't going to have Nyanya
stealing his precious cigars, if he could help it. What
could he do? All day he was trying to think of some
scheme by which he could outwit the clever Nyanya;
and by evening he had hit on a plan. He took a cigar,
made a slit in it, filled the slit with a pinch of gun-
powder, and closed up the slit again with a paper
pellet. He put this cigar back in the box, removed all
the others, locked up the box again, and hung the key
in the usual place.

Then he waited.

For two days, nothing happened. Had Nyanya
seen through the trick? It almost looked as if he had.

Did the cigar perhaps smell different to Nyanya's sensitive nostrils? Mr Oberjohann saw him wander into the tent once or twice; but the cigar still lay in the box...

Perhaps Nyanya *did* suspect something; and perhaps, even so, the temptation was too strong, and he decided to take the risk. At any rate, on the afternoon of the third day, Mr Oberjohann, watching from a distance, saw Nyanya saunter up to his tent, and peep cautiously through the opening. No one was inside. Nyanya walked in. Mr Oberjohann came a little nearer – and waited.

Suddenly – a loud bang, a louder howl! Out dashed Nyanya, yelling and howling, with every hair on his body standing on end. He didn't even glace at Mr Oberjohann; still howling, he rushed past him, bolted into the old man's hut, took him in his arms, and clung to him desperately.

'You are my only friend,' he seemed to be babbling. 'My one and only friend! As for that fellow and his cigars – don't let me ever set eyes on him again!'

But a few days later, he seemed to have forgotten all about it. At dinner-time, he came in and took his seat at Mr Oberjohann's table, in a dignified but friendly manner. Mr Oberjohann was touched. When the meal was over, he opened the precious cigar box, and invited Nyanya to help himself. With a shriek of rage, Nyanya leaped to his feet, seized the table in his two great hands, shook it furiously, flung it over, and, to the sound of crashing crockery and splintering glass, rushed howling from the tent. 'No more of your horrid cigars for me, thank you!'

Nor would he ever touch another.

Soon after this, Mr Oberjohann had to go back to Europe with a cargo of animals. He left the old man

in charge of the camp, and, of course, left Nyanya
with him. He was away two months, and during that
time he often thought of Nyanya. How would Nyanya
behave when he got back? Would he be sulky with
him for having gone away and left him? Or would he,
perhaps, even have forgotten him, and treat him like
a stranger? He did so hope Nyanya would remember
him, and be friendly!

And Nyanya *did* remember him, and he *was*
friendly. He was more than friendly. Directly Mr
Oberjohann set foot in the camp again, Nyanya
rushed to him, flung his arms round his neck, and
hugged him tightly.

But what was this? Nyanya was sobbing like a
child!

'What is it, Nyanya? What's the matter, old
fellow?' asked Mr Oberjohann.

Nyanya couldn't tell him. He only clung to Mr
Oberjohann, and sobbed and sobbed.

'Him lost him's father,' said the head hand. 'Old
man him dead, last fortnight.'

So that was it! The old man, who had loved and
protected Nyanya since he was a baby, had died. And,
for the last fortnight, poor Nyanya had been feeling
that he hadn't a friend left in the world.

'Yes, but you still have a friend, Nyanya,' said Mr
Oberjohann. 'I've come back to you, and I won't
leave you again.'

Nyanya's only answer was a sad little sob, and
another hug.

From that day, Nyanya lived with Mr Oberjohann
in his tent, and shared his bed at night, sleeping always
with one arm flung round him. He still wanted his own
way in everything, and flew into rages if he couldn't

have it; but his love for Mr Oberjohann was boundless, and one day he proved it.

From time to time, Mr Oberjohann would set out on trapping expeditions into the jungle; and though formerly at such times he had left Nyanya at the camp with the old man, now Nyanya refused to stay behind. He was not going to let Mr Oberjohann out of his sight! He rolled his blanket up into a sausage, put it in a basket, and took his place amongst the porters. So, when the expedition set out, there was Nyanya, trotting along with the rest, carrying the basket on his back, keeping it in place with one hand, and helping himself along with a stick held in the other hand. The porters were going at a pace that was rather too quick for him; but he was determined to keep up – that was why he was using a stick.

Now the porters that Mr Oberjohann had hired for this particular expedition turned out to be a bad lot. They stole from him continually, every one of them flatly denying the thefts when questioned. At the end of the first week, when they were deep in the lonely jungle, they came crowding round Mr Oberjohann, demanding their wages.

'No,' says Mr Oberjohann, 'nobody will get any wages, until you give back what you have stolen from me...'

It all happened in a moment. The porters leaped upon him, flung him down, pulled out their knives, and were about to murder him, when, with a roar of rage, Nyanya rushed to the rescue. Seizing hold of two huge men, one in each arm, he sent them crashing against a tree trunk. Then he turned upon the others.

But there were no others. They had fled in all

directions, leaving Nyanya to beat his mighty chest with his fists, and dance, and shout his triumphant 'Ho-a! Ho-a!' whilst Mr Oberjohann got stiffly to his feet again.

How could he ever desert Nyanya after that?

And yet he must return to Europe with another cargo of animals, and there was no one now with whom he could safely leave Nyanya. Then what was he to do? Take Nyanya to Europe with him? Yes, but how could he leave at large, in the cities he must visit, a huge and wilful gorilla, who flew into blind rages if he did not get his own way, and was as ready to kill those who thwarted him, as to protect those whom he loved?

There was only one thing for it. If Nyanya would not go back to his native forest (and it was certain that he would not, for he had lost all sense of how wild gorillas lived) then Nyanya must be taken to Europe in a cage.

2. NYANYA GOES TO EUROPE

So, feeling very like a traitor, Mr Oberjohann began to build a huge cage. And Nyanya watched him.

Nyanya knew all about cages. They were places where you kept lizards and leopards and cobras. Sometimes, too, if you were going on a long journey, you put monkeys in them, and also chimpanzees, and mandrills, and baboons. But you did not put *people* in cages. And when Nyanya went on long journeys, he went like other people, carrying his bundle on his back, and his stick in his hand. So, naturally, the cage had nothing to do with *him*.

Yet, when that cage was finished, Mr Oberjohann

had it carried into his tent. *Their* tent! What now? Was some tiresome animal going to share their tent with them? Nyanya didn't like the idea at all! He followed Mr Oberjohann about anxiously until bed-time came, and then Mr Oberjohann took him by the hand, and they went into the tent together.

The cage was still empty, and the door of it was wide open. Why was it there, then? Nyanya felt frightened. He glanced at Mr Oberjohann anxiously ...

And then, suddenly, his whole world, everything he believed in, and trusted, and loved, crashed in ruins.

'In with you, Nyanya, you're going to sleep in here tonight.'

Nyanya snatched his hand from Mr Oberjohann, crouched in a desolate heap on the floor, and stared into the distance with a dazed, vacant expression. No, he would not look at the hateful cage, he would not look at the deceitful Mr Oberjohann, he would look at nothing and nobody; he would sit where he was, and die.

'Come on, come on, old fellow!' ... That was the deceiver's voice speaking. 'You've got to go into the cage, so you might as well go quickly.'

Was it possible? The friend in whom he had trusted, in whose bed he slept all night, holding him safely in his arms; this man whom he had so loved, whose life he had saved, for whom he would willingly have died! No, it was not possible. Nyanya didn't understand, and he wasn't going to understand; he only knew that he was utterly forsaken, utterly miserable, that nothing mattered any more. And so he still sat, crouched and motionless, with his blank eyes staring into space.

'Come, come *on*! In you go!'

Nyanya sat motionless.

'It's no good your being stubborn. I'm sorry about it, Nyanya, but *you have to go in*!' Mr Oberjohann gave the crouched body a push.

Nyanya still sat motionless.

Mr Oberjohann pushed harder, and began to scold.

Nyanya rose to his feet, gave Mr Oberjohann one reproachful look – and knocked him flat! And then, what a beating Mr Oberjohann got! Before Nyanya had finished with him, his clothes were torn to shreds, and he had wounds that would scar him for life. And yet he didn't attempt to protest, or to defend himself. He understood only too well what Nyanya was feeling. When at last Nyanya let him go, he just got up, and went out to bathe his wounds and put on some fresh clothes. And when he came back into the tent again, he found Nyanya sitting as before, crouched, desolate, staring with blank eyes at nothing.

'Nyanya,' said Mr Oberjohann gently, 'if you won't go into the cage, will you go back and live with your own kind in the forest? I don't want to keep you against your will. You have lived with me freely, and you shall go as freely. Say good-bye now, and go!'

Nyanya raised his head then, and looked Mr Oberjohann full in the eyes. What was passing through his unhappy mind? Mr Oberjohann could only guess. The next thing that happened was that Nyanya held out his hand, took Mr Oberjohann's for a moment, dropped it – and staggered of his own accord into the cage.

And in that cage he sat and sobbed, as though his heart was broken.

It seemed, indeed, as if his heart *was* broken. Mr Oberjohann left the cage door open, but Nyanya would not come out of it. Nor would he eat. Day after day he sat in a corner of the cage with his arms folded, and his head bowed, as much to say, 'There is no use in my living any longer – leave me to die.'

'Come for a walk with me, Nyanya,' pleaded Mr Oberjohann at last.

Nyanya got up obediently and came out of the cage. He let Mr Oberjohann take his hand and lead him where he would. But he walked with bowed head, and looked at nothing. And, when they got back to the tent, he went straight into his cage, and crouched himself down in the corner again.

Mr Oberjohann coaxed and petted and fondled him, offered him dainties to eat, praised him, tried to explain to him. It was all no good, he might have been talking to a dummy; not one gleam of expression came into Nyanya's vacant eyes. The time when Mr Oberjohann must leave for Europe, with his cargo of animals, was drawing nearer and nearer. What on earth was he to do? If only he could think of some way of stirring Nyanya's spirits back to life! But he could think of no way.

And then, when Mr Oberjohann was really in despair, an impudent crow worked the miracle, and saved Nyanya's life.

One day, hand in hand, Nyanya and Mr Oberjohann came back from their melancholy walk – Nyanya with bowed head as usual. And in the cage, perched on the food table, was a crow, cramming its maw with all the dainties that Nyanya had refused even to look at. Nyanya knew this crow; in happier days it had often come stealing food from him, and he had raged and scolded and tried to catch it, but always it was too cunning for him. Now, at sight of it, a flash of anger glittered in Nyanya's deep-set eyes: glittered – and vanished again, leaving them expressionless as ever. But he had at least felt *something*, and Mr Oberjohann was overjoyed. He led Nyanya into the cage, sat down by him, and flung his arms about him.

'Nyanya, Nyanya, Nyanya! Pull yourself together, old man! You are going to get better, do you hear? *You are going to get better!*'

Nyanya went slowly over to the table, picked up some food, looked at it, and put it down. Was he going to eat, or wasn't he? Mr Oberjohann went out and left him. When he came back in the evening, Nyanya was sitting motionless in his corner again, but on the floor of the cage was a strew of orange and apple and banana skins, grape pips, carrot and potato peelings, and crumbs of bread. He had got his appetite back, he had eaten a good meal!

So Nyanya recovered his health, but not yet his spirits. He could not forget that he was no longer a free and useful person, but an animal caged for transport like all the other animals. When the day of transportation came, his cage was covered with thick matting, and the door was locked; and it was as a prisoner, sitting in darkness, that he took the long journey across country to the port. Why was he in darkness, one might ask. Because Mr Oberjohann did not want to have curious crowds staring at him, and making him feel more of a prisoner than ever. But when they reached the port, and it was dusk, and the curious crowds had gone home, Mr Oberjohann opened the cage door, and called him.

'Come out, and take a look round you, Nyanya. You've never seen such sights in all your life! Houses and cars, and ships and cranes! Just you come out and have a look!'

Nyanya came out. Slowly his eyes moved from one

strange object to another: he felt scared. A solitary gorilla in a new and alarming world . . . He turned and looked at Mr Oberjohann. He looked at him for a long, long time. Then, suddenly, he rushed to him, took him in his arms, and hugged him to his breast:

'*You*, at least, are not strange! I still have *you*! Though you do things I can't understand, I believe that you are still my friend!'

And so, having given Mr Oberjohann a tremendous hug, Nyanya at last released him, and began to dance for joy!

Now he had recovered his spirits, as well as his health, and the sea voyage was one long delight to him. He had the run of the ship, only going into his cage at night to sleep. He was happy as happy could be, because he was once more a *person*, who had duties to do, and was making himself useful. His duties were to look after Mr Oberjohann's cargo of monkeys, to clean out their cages, and take them their meals. And how he swept and scrubbed and scoured those cages! All the people on board gathered round to watch him; he worked from morning till night; and when bed-time came, he could hardly keep his eyes open; he would go into his cage and fall asleep at once. But, however sleepy he might be, he never forgot to give Mr Oberjohann a good-night hug, before he went to bed.

When they arrived in Europe, Mr Oberjohann, having seen all his other animals safely off the ship, locked Nyanya in his cabin, and went to call on a friend of his. This friend was a dealer in wild animals – would he look after Nyanya for a little while, until he could be safely housed in the city zoo? The friend said he would, and went back to the ship with Mr Oberjohann. Nyanya was in a very cheerful mood; he shook hands with Mr Oberjohann's friend, and they all three left the ship together.

'He'll be all right with me,' said the friend. 'I know all there is to know about wild animals.'

'You may know all there is to know about lions and tigers,' Mr Oberjohann warned him. 'But that doesn't mean that you understand how to deal with a gorilla. It has taken me eight years to learn how to handle the big apes. Now, take my advice: treat Nyanya as a human being, and he will be your friend. But never, never let him think that you regard him merely as an animal; if you do – look out for yourself!'

The friend laughed. 'Oh, we shall get on famously!' he said.

Night came; they found a big, empty bear's cage for Nyanya to sleep in, and Nyanya, who had been getting used to all sorts of strange things lately, didn't seem to mind. Mr Oberjohann said good night to him, and went away. Nyanya rolled himself in a blanket, and fell peacefully asleep.

But in the morning, when he awoke, he stared about him in astonishment. His cage was in the centre of a large hall, and all round him were other cages, full of wild animals. And, in a cage near him, he saw his most hated, his most deadly enemy – a leopard!

All apes and monkeys detest leopards, and they have good reason to; for the leopard is crafty as a fox, and agile as a monkey itself, and it can climb like a cat, and even high in a tree, a monkey is not safe from its clutches. And though grown-up gorillas are more than a match for it any day, their babies are at its mercy, should they stray from their mothers. And so the feeling of the gorilla tribe towards the leopards is one of deep, deep hatred.

A leopard! Nyanya glared. He sprang up and stood erect; his hair bristled all over his body; he seized two bars of his cage in his huge hands and bent them apart as easily as if they had been bamboo twigs. He leaped out. Howling with rage, he thumped his breast with both his fists; then he made a rush. Inside the cages the other animals began to bound about in fright; lions roared, wolves howled, hyenas laughed like maniacs, cranes screamed, zebras hee-hawed and stamped. Nyanya picked up the cages in his arms and hurled them pell-mell at the leopard. Crash! Crash! Crash! The place was a roaring, howling, ear-splitting pandemonium!

Mr Oberjohann's friend, awakened by the uproar, rushed into the hall. Quickly he dragged the leopard's cage outside into the courtyard. Then he came running back, waving a pitchfork.

'Treat him like a human being!' He had forgotten Mr Oberjohann's warning. And, indeed, how could he be expected to treat a mad gorilla like a human being? He went for Nyanya with the pitchfork. Nyanya seized an iron bar, smashed the handle of the pitchfork with one blow, and bit Mr Oberjohann's friend in the shoulder. The man fled. Nyanya followed, caught up with him at the door, and lammed into him with the iron bar. The man just managed to get out and slam the door behind him. Then he staggered into the courtyard and dropped unconscious.

A crowd gathered. The police were sent for, and came in two squads, armed with rifles and pistols. In the hall, behind the closed door, the uproar was still going on. The police were about to enter in a body and shoot Nyanya, when Mr Oberjohann's friend recovered consciousness.

'No, no, *no*, don't shoot him!' he gasped. 'It's all

my fault – I made a mistake! Send for his owner!
Quickly! Quickly!'

As soon as he got the message, Mr Oberjohann
jumped into a taxi, and was driven at top speed
towards the spot. But by this time the crowd was so
huge that the roads about the courtyard were jammed.
A policeman tried to turn the taxi back – 'Can't you
see the road's blocked?' Mr Oberjohann leaped out,
thrust the policeman aside, and struggled on. What
was happening beyond the courtyard? Would he ever
reach Nyanya...?

And then, suddenly, somewhere in front of him, he
heard a loud roar, so loud a roar that all the houses
echoed it: 'Ho-a! Ho-a!' Nyanya's triumphant
war-cry!

'Hoo-ee! Hoo-ee! Hoo-ee!' roared Mr Oberjohann
in reply.

The crowd was now stampeding from the courtyard. 'The gorilla's out! The gorilla's out!' Everyone
was shouting and running. Nyanya had broken
through the police cordon, and the police, too, were
running. In a courtyard empty of all but their two
selves, Nyanya and Mr Oberjohann met and
embraced.

Nyanya was in high glee. 'I showed them a thing
or two, didn't I? I made them run, didn't I? Here we
are together again! And what next?'

Yes, indeed, what next? Mr Oberjohann's friend,
with his head swathed in bandages, and looking very
sick and sorry for himself, came shakily back into the
courtyard.

'Take him away, for mercy's sake!' he said, keeping
well out of reach of Nyanya. 'Yes, I know it was all my
fault; but I never want to set eyes on a gorilla again as
long as I live!'

Mr Oberjohann took Nyanya by the hand, and led him out of the courtyard. 'Well, as you so truly said, Nyanya, here we are together again, but — ' Then he remembered another friend of his in the city, Herman, the snake-charmer. Perhaps Herman would house Nyanya for a day or two? Anyway he could but try. So he hailed a taxi.

The taxi-driver looked very doubtful.

'It's all right,' said Mr Oberjohann, 'I promise he'll be good.'

And he pushed Nyanya into the back of the taxi, and sat down beside him.

And, at first, Nyanya *was* good. He peered through the window, and seemed amused at the sensation he was causing. Then he became interested in the driver's hands on the steering wheel.

'Look, Nyanya, look!' cried Mr Oberjohann, trying to interest him in something else. 'There's a woman carrying a basket, I believe it's got eggs in it! And — look! there's a little boy waving to you! And...'

Nyanya took not the slightest notice. He stared and stared at the steering wheel. Suddenly, at a busy cross-roads, he shot out one long arm, and seized the wheel himself. The driver, in a terrible fright, switched off the engine, the car skidded half across the road, and came to a halt in the middle of it, all but overturning.

'Go on, go on, what are you stopping for?' Nyanya climbed into the front seat. But the driver wouldn't go on; so Nyanya pushed him out of the car, and took his seat at the wheel. He pressed his long fingers on to one button after another, he twiddled the wheel, he crashed the gear-lever, he stamped on the pedals, he honked and honked at the horn. The car would *not* go on!

'Now then, now then,' says a policeman. 'What's all this about?'

'Oh, just a temporary breakdown, officer,' says Mr Oberjohann.

'But – but what's that at the wheel?'

'My ape, officer.'

Cars were hooting, trams clanging their bells, buses honking; the traffic jam got thicker every moment. Mr Oberjohann seized Nyanya and shouted in his ear.

'It's no use fiddling with those levers, Nyanya. Can't you see we've broken down? Get out, and help push!'

Nyanya got out. He and Mr Oberjohann and the driver and the policeman all pushed together, and got the car against the pavement. The policeman, of course, wanted Mr Oberjohann's name and address. Mr Oberjohann, trying to talk the policeman into a good mood, was keeping an anxious eye on Nyanya. What was he up to now? Oh heavens, he was smashing the window of a fruit shop!

'Hoo-ee! Hoo-ee!' roared Mr Oberjohann.

Nyanya, triumphantly waving a bunch of bananas, rushed back, and hugged him. Out came the angry shop-woman.

'You must pay for all this damage!' she cried.

Mr Oberjohann was going to follow her into the shop, when the policeman stopped him.

'Get back into the taxi,' he said. 'You'll have to come to the police-station.'

'Presently, presently,' said Mr Oberjohann, and walked on towards the shop. The policeman followed, and caught him by the arm.

'You dare touch him!' roared Nyanya, and made a pounce at the policeman.

The policeman fled.
And hand in hand, Mr
Oberjohann and Nyanya
entered the shop.

Mr Oberjohann took
out his note-case and paid
for the broken window.
Then he bought a huge
box full of oranges and
bananas for Nyanya.

'*Now* we'll go to the police-station,' he said.

So, still hand in hand, off they went, Nyanya carrying his box of fruit. It seemed that he had had enough of excitement, and was glad to be quiet. At the police-station he behaved most politely. He made friends with everybody, and, half an hour later, came away without a stain on his character.

And so, at last, they reached the house of Herman, the snake-charmer, where Nyanya put his box of fruit down on the floor, and seated himself comfortably on a sofa. Mr Oberjohann thought it might be safest to put him in a cage; but Herman wouldn't hear of it.

'You leave him to me,' said Herman, 'we'll look after each other.'

'I shan't be long, Nyanya,' said Mr Oberjohann. 'And you *will* be a good boy, won't you?'

'Ho!' answered Nyanya, meaning, 'You know that all depends.'

Still feeling rather anxious, Mr Oberjohann hurried away. He *had* to see the Director of the Zoo; but, goodness me, what might not happen in his absence? He didn't get back till evening. But all was well. He found Herman and Nyanya sitting one on each side of the stove in the dining-room, each smoking a pipe.

The next day Nyanya was safely housed in the city zoo. And, by and by, Mr Oberjohann went back to Africa.

3. NYANYA IN THE ZOO

A year passed. Far away in Africa, Mr Oberjohann thought of his friend, Nyanya. He hated the idea of his being shut up in a zoo. But what else could he have done with him?

'Heaven grant he's settled down, and is happy and contented!' thought Mr Oberjohann.

Then, one day, a boy arrived with a bundle of letters from the post office, which was many days' march from the camp. One of the letters was from the Director of the city zoo. 'Please take your gorilla away,' he wrote. 'Otherwise I shall have to destroy him. He is quite unmanageable.'

Mr Oberjohann immediately sent the boy back two hundred miles with a telegram. 'Do not destroy Nyanya. I am coming.'

By the first ship he could get, he travelled back to Europe. Without letting anyone know he had arrived, he hurried to the zoo, and walked into the monkey house. It was a long hall, with monkey cages all round the walls, and aviaries full of tropical birds arranged down the centre aisle. Mr Oberjohann walked down the hall till he came near to the gorilla's cage. Yes, Nyanya was there, all by himself, behind those thick bars! Mr Oberjohann hid behind one of the aviaries, and watched him.

To and fro, to and fro, behind the bars of his cage, Nyanya was pacing. Each time he came to the end of the bars, he gave a quick glance up and down the alley-way in front of his cage – a space that was reserved for visitors. There was no one there, and he continued his pacing. And then, all at once he stopped, raised himself to his full height, and began to hop from one foot to the other. Then he gripped the bars with his great hands, and shook them.

Mr Oberjohann looked round, and saw an elderly lady walking up to the cage. She came as close as she could to Nyanya, spoke to him, and waved her hand. Nyanya stepped back from the bars, flung his hands above his head, let them fall, and uttered a most piteous cry!

'You see I can't get out,' he was telling her. 'I am trapped in here. I would come to you if I could, but I am trapped, trapped, trapped!'

Then a keeper came along, carrying a truncheon. He went up to the cage, and rattled on the bars with the truncheon. Nyanya, mad with rage, flew at the bars, shook them and tore at them, fell back, stooped, and beat the floor with his fists. Then, frantically, he lowered his head, and charged the wall of his cage with such fury, that he cut his head, and fell to the ground, stunned. When he came round, he put up his hand to his head, in a dazed sort of way, brought it down covered with blood, and began licking the blood off his fingers.

At that moment, the elderly lady caught sight of Mr Oberjohann, and hurried over to him. She was crying.

'You see how they are treating him!' she cried. 'I can't bear it! I've been to the Director and implored him to let me buy Nyanya. I've been many times. He thinks I'm mad. He won't listen to me. That keeper is a brute! He has a grudge against the gorilla. One morning, when he brought him his food, Nyanya refused it. The keeper got angry, and threatened him with the truncheon. Nyanya snatched the truncheon from him, and gave *him* a beating. Another keeper came to his aid, and Nyanya beat him, also. They had to turn the hose on him to stop him. Now that brute of a keeper does all he can to get his own back. And no one dares to go into the cage. They say Nyanya is vicious and must be destroyed. But oh, I know, I *know* he isn't vicious! He's only terribly unhappy! What can I do? The fuss I keep on making has prevented him from being destroyed so far. But I think he will soon die of his own accord, from grief.'

'Madam,' said Mr Oberjohann, 'if you so wish, in an hour from now, you shall walk with Nyanya in the park.'

The lady stared at him, gasped, and stammered, 'In – in – the park? But – but – do you mean that you . . .?'

'Yes,' said Mr Oberjohann. 'It is my fault that he's behind those bars. I am going to free him.'

He hurried away, found a door leading into the keepers' quarters, and so got to the back of Nyanya's cage. There was a trap-door at the back of the cage. The door was locked, but the key was in the lock. Mr Oberjohann was just going to open it, when the keeper rushed up.

'Hi! Stop, stop!' he shouted. 'What are you doing? Keep back! Clear out of here!'

'It is *you* who had better clear out, if you value your life,' said Mr Oberjohann calmly. He turned the key in the trap-door. The keeper fled in terror. Mr Oberjohann opened the door.

'Nyanya!' he called.

When Nyanya heard his voice, he was through that trap-door in a flash. Sobbing and crying with joy, he flung himself into Mr Oberjohann's arms with such force that they both fell to the ground. Mr Oberjohann caressed him, and talked tenderly to him. Hugging Mr Oberjohann to his breast, Nyanya sobbed and sobbed.

When he was a little calmer, Mr Oberjohann took him by the hand, and they walked away from that hated cage together. They walked slowly down through the big monkey hall between the aviaries. By this time a crowd had gathered; and Nyanya, seeing a little girl amongst them, stopped and held out his hand to her. The little girl smiled, and held out *her* hand. Nyanya took it, and held it for a long, long time.

'Come along, Nyanya,' said Mr Oberjohann at last. 'I think your friend is waiting for you in the park.'

The elderly lady *was* waiting for him in the park. Directly he saw her, Nyanya dropped Mr Oberjohann's hand, and ran, and took her in his arms. He laid his head on her shoulder, and gazed into her eyes, whilst she stroked and petted him. She meant more, far more, to Nyanya now than Mr Oberjohann did: *he* had deserted Nyanya for a long, long time, and left him to suffer heart-ache and misery; but *she* had come every day to visit him in his affliction. And because of her visits, through all his misery, he had somehow managed to retain his desire to live.

He let Mr Oberjohann leave him without a protest. Indeed, he scarcely seemed to notice him. He was going home with his friend. Holding her firmly by the hand, Nyanya walked away with her. He was not going to be a caged animal ever again. Once more he was a *person*.

And, as a person, he lived in the lady's house, completely free and entirely happy, for the rest of his life.

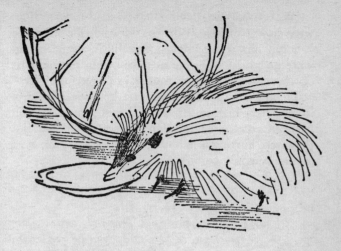

7. *The Hedgehog*

'Wake-wake-wake-wake!'

What was that? A funny little noise in the darkness of the silent meadow. The noise was coming from under our caravan. We got a torch, and flashed it on to the dewy grass between the caravan wheels. It was a hedgehog. But he didn't curl himself into a prickly ball when the light fell on him; he just stayed very still, with the spines on his back lying flat, his little head stuck out, and his long, pointed nose quivering. His front legs, too, were sprawling in an odd manner; and, when we looked close, we saw that he had hurt them. Perhaps he had been caught in a trap, and wrenched himself free; at any rate, those poor little front legs of his were very red and scratched and sore-looking.

69

'Wake-wake-wake-wake!' It seemed to us as if he were crying for help. What could we do for him? We brought him some bread and milk in a saucer, and were delighted when he at once began to gobble it down, champing his jaws loudly, just like a little pig.

When he dipped his nose into the saucer (such a funny, sharp little nose it was!) he rested his weight on his front legs, so we knew they couldn't be broken. But they were hurting him badly, and he was telling us so as plainly as if he could speak.

'Oh dear me, how this left leg of mine hurts!' he way saying, lifting it up and waving it in the air, whilst he took all the weight on his right leg.

'No, no, I made a mistake! This *right* leg of mine hurts worse, *much* worse!' he said. And he put down the left leg, and waved the right one in the air. And so he went on, lifting up one poor little leg and then the other, as if he couldn't decide which hurt him most. But, all the time, he was gobbling up the bread and milk for all he was worth. Until, when the saucer was quite empty, he drew back his head, curled himself up into a ball, with the spines sticking up all over him, and, as we supposed, went to sleep.

In the morning he was still there, and still curled up in exactly the same place, not having moved, so it seemed, all through the night. And all through the day, whenever we went to look at him, there he was, the same little spiky ball in the same place. Was he alive, or was he dead? We couldn't tell.

But in the evening, when we were having our supper, we again heard that funny little cry, 'Wake-wake-wake-wake!' from under the caravan.

And he *was* awake, and calling for *his* supper!

We took him his saucerful of bread and milk; and again he gobbled it up, champing his jaws like a little pig; and again he kept shifting his weight from one sore leg to the other, holding up first the left leg and then the right leg, as if, when both were hurting him so badly, he really couldn't decide which one was worse.

When he had gobbled up all his supper, and not a crumb of bread, or a drop of milk, was left in the saucer, he gave the tiniest little sigh, as much as to say, 'Well, I'm full at any rate, even if my legs do hurt!'

And then he curled himself up into a spiky ball again, and went to sleep.

Every day, for the next week or so, whenever we looked under the caravan, there he was curled up in exactly the same place; he didn't seem to have moved one inch. And every evening, at exactly the same time, he uncurled himself and stuck out his little head. Then it was, 'Wake-wake-wake-wake! Be quick and bring my supper!'

But each evening, we noticed that his legs seemed to be hurting him less and less. He still lifted up first one of them, and then the other, but not so quickly, or impatiently. And then, in about a fortnight, there came an evening when there he was, gobbling up his supper with *both* his forefeet on the ground, as if they weren't hurting him at all!

'Wake-wake-wake-wake!' Next evening he was calling for his supper again. But the call was not coming from under the caravan; it was coming from in front of it. We hurried out, and found him standing by the steps, with his beady eyes peering up at us, and his sharp-pointed nose sniffing the air impatiently. We brought out his bread and milk, and put down the saucer on the grass about two feet away from him, and he immediately trotted over to it, and began to eat in a business-like manner.

'Bad legs?' he seemed to say. 'Oh yes, well, I did

71

once have bad legs. But that's a thing of the past, and truly, until you mentioned it, I'd forgotten all about it!'

That evening, when he had finished his supper, he didn't go back under the caravan, but rambled off into the hedge. And next morning we couldn't see him anywhere. But in the evening he was outside the caravan door again, calling for his supper.

'Wake-wake-wake-wake!' He called us for many evenings. And then, one evening, he didn't call. Nor did we ever see him again. But he was well and strong now, and could fend for himself. And probably, among the grubs and worms and beetles in the meadow, he found food more to the liking of a fine, sturdy, grown-up hedgehog than our pappy bread and milk.

8. *Boney, Molly, and Waddy*

Mr Lockhart was in Singapore with a big circus. One day, as he was taking a stroll through the town, a man came up to him, leading a baby elephant.

'Sahib buy little elephant, most pretty little elephant, cheap little elephant?'

She *was* a pretty little elephant, grey in colour, and about the size of a big dog; her bright little eyes were full of baby mischief – almost it seemed as if she would break out into roguish laughter at any moment. She was so bursting with life and energy that she couldn't keep still. Altogether, she was adorable! Mr Lockhart fell in love with her. He bought her for £37 and took her back to the circus to show to his wife.

'Heavens!' exclaimed Mrs Lockhart. 'But how are we going to feed her? She's so young! I'm sure she can't eat! She needs her mother's milk. Where *is* her mother? Oh, supposing she should die!'

'I think she's an orphan,' said Mr Lockhart. 'Anyway, it's up to us to keep her alive now.'

He sent out for several crates of condensed milk. Mrs Lockhart dipped her fingers into the milk, and offered them to the little elephant to suck.

'Good, good, good!' The little elephant tucked her little trunk up out of the way, shut her eyes, took the milky fingers in her mouth, and sucked and sucked, and chirruped and asked for more. There was going to be no difficulty in keeping *her* alive! And soon she grew big and strong, and was able to eat hay and oats, and bread and carrots, and sugar.

They christened her Borneo; but very soon they found themselves calling her Boney, which sounded more affectionate.

'Boney, Boney, Boney!' Mr Lockhart would call; and up she would come, running, because she knew that Mr Lockhart had a handful of sugar for her. And how she loved sugar! That was the way he taught her all her tricks, by rewarding her with sugar. And she was very quick to learn; not only because she liked sugar, but also because she liked being clever.

She didn't seem to be lonely, but Mr Lockhart thought it would be nice for her to have companions. So, one day, he bought two more little elephants called Molly and Waddy. When Boney saw them, she squealed with delight. Now they were three inseparables! They used to go about in single file, holding each other's tails, with Boney, who was the smallest of them, proudly leading.

Mr Lockhart brought them back to England, and set about training them for a circus act. He taught them to play skittles; with two of them rolling the balls at the skittles with their trunks, and the third setting up the tumbled-down skittles again. They had great fun knocking down those skittles! But it took them a little time to understand the difference between a skittle and a ball. And, at first, they would try to set up a ball amongst the skittles, and get very vexed when it rolled away.

Mr Lockhart also taught them to fire cannons at each other, and to tumble down and sham dead; to see-saw, with one on each end of the board, and one standing in the middle, shifting her weight from side to side to work the board up and down; and to play an elephant band. Boney became quite an accomplished performer in the band. First she learnt to play a mouth-organ, and then to turn a hand-organ; and, by and by, whilst still turning the organ, she would play a cymbal with one forefoot. That was a difficult trick, because she had to learn to keep the rhythm; at first she crashed the cymbal anyhow, and the result was very funny, but rather ear-splitting. However, in the end, she got the idea, and clashed the cymbal to the beat of the tune on the organ.

But the trick the three elephants liked best was the café scene. In this scene, Waddy was dressed as a cook, in a white apron and a huge white hat. Boney was dressed as a clown, and Molly as a policeman. Boney sat on a stool at a table, and rang a bell: ' *Ting-a-ling-a-ling!* Where's my dinner?' Waddy brought in a plate of food and a bottle of 'wine'. But, when Boney had eaten all the food, and tossed off the contents of the bottle, in came Waddy again with a huge bill; and – goodness me! – Boney, though she searched through all her pockets, couldn't find a penny to pay with! So then off marches Waddy for a policeman, and in comes Molly, with an enormous helmet on her head, and a truncheon swinging in her trunk.

Whack, whack, whack! goes Molly with the truncheon, and the naughty Boney is beaten out of the ring.

The elephants all loved this little act, because it made people laugh so heartily, and Molly particularly liked whanging Boney with the truncheon. She liked it so much that she wanted the game to go on; and, when they went back to their stable, she would pick up a hay-band, and go on beating Boney for hours. Of course it didn't hurt, and probably Boney enjoyed it as much as Molly did, or else she would soon have made Molly stop. For though Boney was the smallest

of the three of them, she was the leader and boss.

Then Boney learnt a trick that made her really famous, and that was to ride a tricycle. Mr Lockhart had the tricycle especially made for her, and it was very big and very heavy – it had need to be, to carry an elephant! Instead of handle-bars it had a long tiller, and it had four huge round pedals, bigger than Boney's feet. Boney, who had learnt to sit on stools and see-saws, had no difficulty in climbing into the saddle, and she found out for herself how to fit her feet comfortably into the pedals. Then she took the tiller in her trunk and played with it, moving it this way and that.

But the tricycle itself didn't move – not yet; because Mr Lockhart had put wooden wedges in front and behind each of the wheels, and he kept the wedges there until he was sure that Boney was quite at home in the saddle.

Then, one day, he took away the wedges.

Now what would happen? He felt a little anxious. Would Boney be scared when the tricycle began to move? Would she try to get off, and perhaps upset it? Not a bit of it! With great glee she started pedalling; and when she found that she had only to swing the tiller to make the tricycle go where she wanted, she was triumphant! In ten minutes, so Mr Lockhart tells us, she was blissfully riding round and round.

And, though she didn't know it, she was the very first elephant in the world to ride a tricycle.

Boney, Molly, and Waddy became very famous, and travelled all over the world. One day they were in France, performing on an out-of-doors stage. And, of course, Boney was to do her cycling act. She had become so clever at it, that she could now do figures of eight in the most masterly fashion. But that day it had been raining, and the wooden stage was slippery; and in the midst of one of her figures of eight, the tricycle wheels skidded, and Boney, tricycle and all, went hurtling off the platform, and into the orchestra seated below.

77

The musicians leaped up and ran for their lives, for Boney had landed, *thump!* right on the big drum! But if the musicians were scared, Boney wasn't. She had the situation well in hand. She picked herself up, and gave herself a shake, as much as to say, 'Dear, dear! these little accidents will happen to the cleverest of us!' Then she picked up the tricycle, carefully hoisted it on to the platform, climbed up after it, calmly reseated herself in the saddle, settled her feet comfortably in the pedals, took the tiller in her trunk – and next minute there she was, cycling round and round once more in her figures of eight, as sedately as if nothing had happened!

9. *The Bull*

'You needn't be afraid of *my* bull, ma'am,' says Farmer Nicholls. 'He's gentle as a lamb, and never hurt no one in his life. Some bulls *is* savage, I'll admit; but not he. It's the way you treat 'em makes all the difference. I never did hold with keeping a bull tied up; I lets mine run with the cows, winter and summer. And when a bull's *with* the cows, he's content. If *you* was to be shut away all by yourself, and never see no company, you'd soon feel like rampaging, wouldn't you? Stands to reason. Well, it's the same with bulls. And that's what my neighbour over yonder won't understand.

'Tom Job is my neighbour's name. He's a bachelor, and has his three sisters living with him. Always at him, they are, about this and that, cackling away like three old hens. So maybe,' (Farmer Nicholls chuckled), 'neighbour Job sometimes feels he'd rather be shut away by *himself*. Anyways, that's what he does with his bull, all the winter through. It's the savagest animal in all the seven parishes; and when it does come out to graze in spring, it goes about with a ring in its nose and a monstrous heavy chain dangling. I feel sorry for it, that I do! And the only person that can handle it, without danger to himself, is daft Eddy.

'Daft Eddy is a lad that works for them. He's not so daft but that he can do a good day's work, or you may be sure they wouldn't employ him. But he moves slow, and he speaks slow, when he does speak, which isn't often. And he looks a bit dazed, like. So they get his work cheap; and that means a lot to 'em, for the whole four of 'em, brother and sisters alike, are stingy-minded.

'Well now, last winter they had that bull tied up in a shed, as usual. Tied up very short by the head, he was, so they could go in and out, and feed him. They're very clean sort of people, and that shed was white-washed fit to dazzle a body. And you fancy, ma'am, the bull a-staring at that white wall, so close up to his eyes, all the winter long, and not being able to turn his head away from it! You could hear him bellowing from our farm, night and day; and, come spring, he was like a raging lunatic. Who wouldn't be?

'And then one morning, in March last it was, and they were thinking to let him out, they find he'd worked his halter off his head. And when Tom Job went in, the animal turns round and charges him. He only just gets out of the door in time to bang it after him, and save his skin.

'So there they were; the bull inside, a-banging at the shed walls with his horns, and bellowing, and they outside, women and all; all giving tongue together, and shouting out what should be done, and no one listening to what t'others said, and no one doing nothing. One says, "Shoot him", and another says, "Send for the police", and another says, "Send for Farmer Nicholls". But I ask you – what could I have done? I'm no more fit to deal with mad bulls than anyone else is. All *I* know is how to keep 'em from *going* mad.

'Well, in the midst of this here uproar – bellowings from within the shed, and shoutings outside of it, and the wooden wall of the shed swaying and bending when the bull ran against it, like as if he was going to break through and murder them all – in the midst of all this, up strolls daft Eddy, with that slow walk of his, and the dazed expression on his face. He goes up to that slammed door, opens it a crack, and peeks in.

'"Keep back!" roars Tom Job. "You fool, what d'you think you're doing of? Shut that door, I tell you!"

'But Eddy seemed to have turned deaf – he didn't shut that door; leastways not till he'd opened it wide enough to slip inside, and shut it behind him. What happened then? I don't know; only that the bull stopped bellowing, and there was a silence, except that one of the women began to cry. And then, by and by, out comes daft Eddy, leading the bull by the halter, which he'd put over its head again, and the bull following quiet, though drooling at the mouth, and rolling its eyes wild. And those folk scattering in all directions, something comical.

'"Where'll I put him?" asks daft Eddy.

'"Anywhere you like," shouts Tom Job, from top the hedge, where he's scrambled.

'So Eddy leads him off to the field where the cows were, and the poor beast stands there shivering and looking round him, most as dazed in the face as daft Eddy himself. And would you believe it, ma'am, what Tom Job said, when he was safely back in his farm kitchen?

'"Daft Eddy," says he, "he's too stupid to know a bull's horns from its tail, and so, of course, he's too stupid to feel afraid of it."

'Yes, you may well laugh! Fact is, daft Eddy's got something about him that other folk haven't, and animals know it. When he walks up through the fields, there isn't a cow but turns her head to look after him. Aye, I've seen it many's the time. And it makes you wonder.'

10. *Billy, the Little Military Learned Horse*

Just about two hundred years ago, there lived a young lad called Philip Astley. Philip's father was a cabinet maker, and he thought Philip ought to be a cabinet maker also. But Philip didn't like cabinet making; what *he* liked was horses. And all the time whilst he was sawing and hammering, screwing and glueing amongst the shavings in his father's workshop, he was thinking of the ride he had had last week-end, or the ride he was going to have next week-end, or of some particularly beautiful horse he had seen in such-and-such a livery stable, or of the handsome American trotter that young Lord So-and-so was driving yesterday in the park.

And whilst he was thinking such thoughts as these, the saw would slip, the screw go in crooked, and the glue boil over in the pot; and when these things happened, Philip's father would take up a stick, and thrash him, good and hard.

Philip didn't like being thrashed, any more than he liked cabinet making; so one day, when he was seventeen, he borrowed a horse and rode away from his father's house, and enlisted in Colonel Elliot's new regiment, the 15th Dragoons, as a horse-breaker.

The other soldiers were full of admiration for Philip's riding; they had never seen anything like it. Philip would set his horse at a gallop, and somersault off its back, and on to its back again, and off again, and on again, with the horse going full pelt all the time; he would stand up in the saddle and career around, just as easily as if he were standing on firm ground; he would ride standing astride two galloping horses, and put them to jump over fences; he would ride with only one foot on the saddle, and the toe of the other foot in his mouth; and, more surprising than all, he would sometimes be standing on his *head* in the saddle, instead of on his feet.

It was just like the cleverest riding you see nowadays in the circus; but in those days there *were* no circuses – no wonder people were astonished!

When Philip was nineteen years old, his regiment went overseas, to serve under the King of Prussia; and Philip, who was now over six feet in height and of tremendous strength, and splendidly handsome, proved himself a very brave soldier. He had a dare-devil courage that seemed afraid of nothing. In a terrific storm at sea, he swam after and rescued a horse that had fallen overboard; in one battle, finding himself alone and surrounded by the enemy, he wrenched the enemy standard from the man who was carrying it, and, bawling at the top of his extra-loud voice, brought it back triumphant, to lay it at the feet of King George II. In another battle, still all alone, for he would never wait for the rest of the troops to come up, he lifted the wounded Duke of Brunswick on his back, and carried him to safety. Huge, handsome Sergeant-Major Astley, with his bawling voice, and his dare-devil courage, became one of the celebrities in the regiment.

But though Philip had galloped away from his father's workshop to join the army, and though he was winning such renown for himself as a soldier, he didn't really want to be a soldier, any more than he wanted to be a cabinet maker. And so, when he was twenty-four years old, he applied for his discharge, and got it.

He got something else, too, which was far more

important to him than his discharge; he got a present from his colonel and the present was a beautiful white charger, called Gibraltar. So, taking Gibraltar with him, he went back to London, and set up as a horse-breaker.

But horse-breaking wasn't really what he wanted to do, either. What *did* he want to do? He wasn't quite sure.

One day he went to Smithfield market to look around; and what did he see there but a tiny little pony. The pony had a shaggy coat, and very bright, impudent eyes, a flowing mane, and a long tail that swept his fetlocks, and he was so small that the top of his head did not reach the level of Philip's hips. Philip went over and spoke to him, and the pony tossed his little head, rubbed his muzzle against Philip's leg, and gave him an impudent look, as much as to say, 'Well, what about you and me making our way together in the world?'

'The very idea!' says Philip. 'So we will!'

He felt in his pocket to see how much money he had. Five golden sovereigns, that was all, And there were just a few more sovereigns at home in a shabby purse. Yes, he was a poor man. That didn't matter! Have that pony he must and would! And, after a lot of bargaining, he got the pony for his five sovereigns, and led him proudly out of the market, feeling as rich as a king.

Now, at last, Philip knew what he wanted to do. Horse-breaking? Pooh! Anyone could do that! *He* was going to do what no one else had ever done: he was going to found the first circus in the world. He would begin by giving exhibitions of trick-riding on Gibraltar, and training the tiny little pony to perform on his own; and after that – oh, he would have hundreds of horses, and hundreds of ponies, and hundreds of other animals! He could picture it all, how it was going to be – a dazzling, glittering, wonderful show, such as people had never seen before!

Of course it would take time, and a lot of hard work; but Philip wasn't afraid of that. Nothing was too difficult, and nothing was impossible, once you had made up your mind.

'I am no man of straw,' said Philip to himself. 'And what I want to do, I can do.'

And so he began by clipping the little pony's shaggy coat, and grooming him till he shone like a polished chestnut. He christened him Billy, the Little Military Learned Horse, and began teaching him tricks.

It really was astonishing how quickly that bright-eyed little Billy learned. He learned to dance, to jump through hoops, and lie down and pretend to be dead. He learned to count, scraping the ground with his hoof till he came to the right number. He learned to play hide and seek, to wash his feet in a pail of water, to saddle and unsaddle himself, undoing and doing up the saddle girth with his teeth, and – his very cleverest trick, of which Philip was enormously proud – he learned to lay a tea table, lift a kettle of boiling water off the fire, and make tea. Perhaps there wasn't another pony in the whole of creation who could do that!

In the beginning, Philip Astley's first circus in the world was merely a piece of field, ringed round with ropes and stakes. Before each performance, Philip, looking very handsome in full uniform, and mounted on his white charger, Gibraltar, rode round through the streets in the neighbourhood, giving out handbills, and bawling at the top of his very loud voice that the show was about to 'com-*mence*'. Then when a crowd had gathered about the ringed-off enclosure, the same loud voice would be bawling about the turns they were going to see. And when the show was over, this first-of-all-circus-proprietors went round with the hat. Money came tumbling into the hat. It was only pence and halfpence, to be sure, but pence and halfpence, if there are enough of them, make pounds: and Philip Astley prospered. He bought more horses, he bought more ponies, he bought other animals; he had a great love for all animals, and a great understanding of them, but he loved his Little Military Learned Horse, Billy, more than all others.

By and by, he had enough money to open a large building. He called this building The Amphitheatre. Astley's Amphitheatre became very popular, people flocked to see the shows there, and Philip became a rich man.

Now that he was rich, Philip drove about London in his own carriage, and always he had a companion sitting up in the carriage with him. Who was that companion? Why, none other than the Little Military Learned Horse, Billy, to be sure. There he was, perched on the seat like a tiny king, with his four little shining hoofs stuck out neatly in front of him, and his saucy, plumed head nodding a greeting to the admiring crowds.

In London at that time there lived an old showman called Abraham Saunders, who was very down on his luck. Just as everything went well with Philip Astley, so everything went badly with Abraham Saunders. He got deeper and deeper into debt, and one day he told Astley that he just didn't know which way to turn.

'Tell you what,' says Astley, 'I'll lend you my Little Military Learned Horse, Billy, for a week or so. *He'll*

bring the folk crowding into your show, never fear! And when he's earned you enough money to pay off your debts, you must bring him back to me.'

Old Saunders wept with joy. 'Now,' thinks he, 'my fortune's made!'

But alas and alas! Before even Billy could make his fortune for him, the bailiffs called on poor old Saunders, and carried him off to prison for debt. Everything he possessed was sold – and Billy was sold along with the rest!

Philip Astley was in a terrible way. Billy, the Little Military Learned Horse, his pride and joy, seemed to have vanished off the face of the earth. No one knew what had become of him; no one could find him. Yes, of course he had been sold. But to whom? Nobody could say.

The great show in Astley's Amphitheatre went on as usual, with its performing horses and dogs, and wild beasts, and clowns, and riders, and acrobats, and it still seemed as splendid as ever, except to Philip Astley. But for him it wasn't the same show at all, without his beloved little Billy; and when he drove about London in his carriage, with an empty seat beside him, he was as sad as sad could be.

And then one day, two of the performers from the circus were going for a stroll, when they saw, standing outside a public house, a tiny little pony harnessed to a tumbledown vegetable cart. The little pony's shaggy coat was dirty and ungroomed, his little hoofs were plastered with mud, his mane and tail were tangled. But surely, surely it was Billy – of course it was! What other pony in the world had such bright, impudent

89

eyes, or such a roguish way of tossing his little head?
They would know him anywhere!

'Hullo, Billy!' says one.

'Aren't you going to dance for us, Billy?' says the
other.

And immediately, up goes the little pony on his hind
legs, and down he comes again, and begins to dance
about the road, cart or no cart. He waltzes, he polkas,
he capers and skips. Snap goes a shaft, half-over goes
the cart, out roll the vegetables, a crowd gathers. Billy
dances on and on, with the broken cart clattering
after him, and everybody laughing and cheering.

'Enough, enough, Billy!' say the two performers
and Billy comes to a stand. He looks at them out of the
corners of his eyes, and nods his head, as much as to
say, 'Yes, it's Billy right enough. And now, what are
you going to do about it?'

The two men went into the pub, and there they
found Billy's new owner enjoying his mug of beer, and
quite indifferent to what had been going on outside.
They tell him they have come to take Billy back to
Astley's. They offer him all the money they have, quite
a lot of money; and if that isn't enough, they promise
him more: only *they must have Billy*!

'Oh werry well,' said Billy's new owner. 'You can
'ave 'im. I'm not so particular set on 'im ... See 'ere,'
says he, as he pockets the money, 'it's this way. That
pony, I'm not denying that he's a werry good-
tempered little crittur; but he's so full of tricks that we
calls him The Mountebank. And, in our line of
business, mountebanking is a 'andycap.'

And so The Mountebank was unharnessed from the
broken cart, and led in triumph back to Astley's.

You may be sure that he was never lent to anyone
again. Once more he was clipped and groomed and

fondled and petted. Once more he took his seat in the carriage beside Philip Astley, and once more his place in the circus ring. He lived to the good old age of forty-two years, and he kept his roguish looks and his playful ways to the end of his life.

11. *Ma Shwe*

Elephant Bill, as they called Mr Williams, was in
Burma, looking after the elephants that worked in the
teak trade. Teak trees grow best amongst mountains,
where tractors can't be used, and that's where the
elephants come in. Men cut down the trees, and saw
them into logs, and then the elephants push the logs
to the nearest stream. The logs lie in the shallow water,
waiting for the heavy rains that turn the little streams

into raging torrents; the torrents lift the logs, and float them away, miles and miles away downstream, till they reach a river, where they are collected and built into rafts and carried down to some big sea-port, such as Rangoon or Mandalay. It takes a whole year for the teak to reach Rangoon from the place where it is cut down; and all the time the men back in the mountains are busy cutting down more trees, and the elephants are busy pushing the logs into the streams.

Elephant Bill had seventy of these elephants to look after. The elephants worked in groups of seven, in ten different camps; and Elephant Bill spent his time travelling from one camp to the other, examining his elephants to see if they were fit, and doctoring those that might have fallen sick. All these elephants were his friends, and he loved them. He thought elephants were the wisest and the most lovable of all beasts. And here is a story he tells about one of them.

The heavy rains had begun, and Elephant Bill was camped on a river bank. The river had been but a thin trickle of water a few days ago, but now it was a roaring, raging flood. In the dusk, Elephant Bill stood outside the camp, listening. Any moment now, he expected to hear the loud bumping and booming and crashing together of the teak logs, as they were whirled downstream from the little creek high up in the mountains.

No sound yet, except the hubbub of the fast-flowing water.

He was standing near the bank of the river, but high above it, for the bank on that side of the river was formed of high, steep rocks. He glanced upstream – no sign of the logs yet. Then he glanced downstream, and across the river, where, on the opposite bank, the rocks lay in flat ridges. As the river raced past these ridges, one after the other they vanished under the leaping waves. Yes, he could tell by that how very fast the water was rising! Soon he would hear that expected roar of the coming timber.

Suddenly he *did* hear a roar, but it was not the timber. It was an elephant! And a very frightened elephant! What could have happened? On the opposite bank some of his men were rushing up and down and shouting. Elephant Bill ran to the very edge of the rocks on his side of the river, and, leaning over and looking down into the water, he saw one of his elephants, Ma Shwe (which means *Miss Gold*), with her baby calf, trapped in the fast-rising water.

The angry torrent was not yet more than six feet deep, though racing with terrific speed, and deepening every moment. Ma Shwe was still in her depth, but the calf was afloat and squealing with terror. Ma Shwe was as close in to the opposite bank as she could possibly get. She was standing stoutly, broadside on to the torrent, keeping the calf on the upstream side of her, and holding it pressed against her huge body. But every now and then, a wave would lift the calf and whirl it away from her; then, exerting every ounce of her immense strength, she would lash out with her trunk, twine it round the calf, draw it back upstream, and press it against her body again. That great body of hers was like a rock amidst the waves of ocean; the racing waters washed over it, and left it standing, with the calf huddled against it, and held tightly in her trunk.

A huge wave – it broke in a splatter of foam over Ma Shwe's body and raced away; another huge wave, and another, and another: buffeted, blinded, desperately trying to keep her footing, Ma Shwe gave a stagger, and before she could regain her balance, the calf was washed clean over her hindquarters, and was whirling away downstream.

Ma Shwe turned and plunged after it. Ahead of her the poor little calf was being whirled about like a cork, and carried farther and farther away. Ma Shwe was struggling to keep her feet on the bottom, but sometimes she, too, was afloat, as, with all her desperate strength, she plunged on and on, after that little tossing grey body that meant more to her than anything else in life.

On the bank above the river, Elephant Bill was watching helplessly. Was the calf already dead? Would Ma Shwe herself be drowned? He could do nothing. No human help was possible; no man could exist for a moment down there in that rage of waters. Ma Shwe was some fifty yards downstream now, close under his side of the river . . . Ah! She had caught up with the calf at last, and had her trunk round it!

On the bank over her head, and about five feet above the level of the flood, was a narrow ledge of rock. With a tremendous effort, Ma Shwe reared on to her hind legs and pushed the calf to stand upon this ledge. Then she fell back exhausted, and the foaming waters swept her away.

But she must fight, fight now for her own life! For how could the calf, trapped there on the narrow ledge of rock, exist without her? She knew well enough that not far down the river from where she was struggling, the waters dropped suddenly into a deep, narrow gorge. And she knew well enough that if she could not save herself before she was carried down over that fall, it would be the end of her, and she would never see her calf again.

She knew something else, too; before the waters reached that gorge, there was just one place where the bank was flat enough for an elephant to scramble ashore. But this flat place was on the opposite side of the river from the rock-shelf where she had placed her calf. What did that matter? Once out of these terrible waters, that were hurling her this way and that, washing over her head, and beating the breath out of her body – once free to breathe, and think, and stand on her feet again, she would surely find some way of getting back to her calf!

As Elephant Bill stood watching on the rocky bank, the distance and the gathering dusk hid away the life-and-death struggle between Ma Shwe and the raging river from his sight.

He hurried along the bank, till he stood above the shelf where Ma Shwe had put her calf. Peering over, he saw the little thing some eight feet below him. The shelf of rock was only just wide enough to hold its feet. It stood shivering, terrified, humped up, pressing its fat little paunch against the bank. Would it be possible to haul it up by ropes? There was no room for a man to stand on the ledge, the calf filled it completely; but a man might be let down in some sort of a cradle, and attach ropes to the calf, and other men might draw it up. It would be worth trying; it would need several men ...

All these thoughts were racing through Elephant Bill's mind, when he suddenly heard what he describes as the grandest sounds of a mother's love he could ever remember. Ma Shwe was out of the water! She had managed to reach that flat place and struggle on shore, and there she was now, careering up along the opposite bank as fast as her legs could carry her, and calling all the time – a loud roar that echoed along the bank, and drew nearer and nearer.

The calf's little ears, that had lain so miserably flat

against its shivering head, cocked up joyfully. Now everything was all right – its mother was coming! The river raged between them, but she was there, she was calling, she would come, *somehow* she would come! It had only to wait, and stop shivering, and be careful not to tumble off the ledge ...

The dusk was deepening. Elephant Bill was still watching. All at once he saw Ma Shwe's head push through a jungle of growths on the opposite bank. And at the same moment, Ma Shwe saw her calf. Through the dusk she could just make out its dim little shape, its body still firmly planted on the ledge where she had put it. Ma Shwe's roar changed into a tremendous purr of pleasure, a loud, rumbling, ecstatic sound that made itself heard even above the tumult of the waters.

Darkness fell. Ma Shwe was still on one side of the river, her calf on the other. From far up the river, now, came the boom and crash of the floating logs, bumping against each other. Rain fell in torrents. Elephant Bill turned and went back to the shelter of the camp. Would the calf stay where it was till morning? Was there anything he could do for it? Or should he leave it all to Ma Shwe? Somehow he felt that Ma Shwe would find a way to get it off that ledge.

But twice before he went to bed, he hurried out in the rain to the river bank, leaned over, and switched on his torch. Yes, the calf was still on its ledge, but the light from the torch seemed to frighten it, and a frightened movement might cause it to fall. Best leave it alone, and see what would happen ...

The story has a very happy ending. In the morning, the flood waters had gone down, and the river was merely a muddy, slow-flowing stream. The calf was gone from its ledge, it was safe with Ma Shwe; they were both ambling happily along the bank on the opposite side of the river. Nobody had seen her, but Ma Shwe must have crossed the river as soon as the waters subsided, lifted the calf from the ledge, and carried it downstream to that flat place where they could both scramble ashore.

The calf had no name as yet. It was only three months old. But when it came to be christened, the natives all agreed that they couldn't find a better name for it than Ma Yay Yee, which means 'Miss Laughing Water'.

12. *Bobo*

I am Bobo, the baboon, and my master is Mahmud, the merry. Mahmud says that he and I are very much alike. I don't mean in looks, but in character. He says that we are both clever rascals, picking up our daily bread in any way we can; and if we pick it up without paying for it, so much the better.

But there is this difference between us, that whereas Mahmud can speak my language, I cannot speak his. Also, though he often puts a pencil into my hand and says, 'Come on now, Bobo, let's see you write!' I find I can do nothing but make scribbles. So, though it is I who am telling this story, it is Mahmud who is turning it into his own language, and setting it down.

There is another difference between us, too, in that I work harder than Mahmud, who doesn't see why he should work at all. It is by my going through my tricks in the market place, or wherever a crowd is gathered together, that we earn enough for our dinner, when we can't come by that dinner in any other way.

This morning there wasn't anything in the larder, so off we go together to the market; and as soon as a crowd gathered about us, I went through my tricks. I did them well; and Mahmud smiled and nodded and said funny things to make the people laugh, and quite a shower of small coins was thrown into the hat, when I went round holding it out at the end of my performance.

Mahmud took the coins out of the hat, put the hat

back on his head, and rattled the coins together in his hand.

'Now, Bobo,' says he, 'I'm off to get something for dinner. Maybe you'll find *your* dinner hereabouts.'

And he gives me a wink, and off he goes.

I looked around, but I didn't see any likelihood of a dinner where I was, so I went off to a quiet corner behind the market, and there I sat on my haunches, holding my tail, which always helps me to think; and prevents naughty boys from pulling it, too. If a naughty boy pulls my tail, I'm apt to get angry and hit out, and when I begin hitting out I don't know when to stop, and that leads to trouble, both for Mahmud and for me. We've got a name for being good-tempered, and I try to live up to it; we don't want trouble, so it's best to keep temptation out of the boys' way. Also, as I said, when I sit comfortably holding my tail, I can think better, because I'm not distracted.

So I held my tail in my hand, and blinked this way and that, keeping a sharp look-out for whatever might chance. I hadn't sat there long when a date-seller passed me, with a bundle under his arm, and a big basket of dates in his hand. He set the basket on the ground under a wall at a little distance from me, sat himself down by it, unrolled his bundle, took out a loaf of bread and a piece of meat, and began to eat. Watching him eat made me feel hungry. I looked at the basket of dates, and thought to myself, *There's* my dinner!

Should I go over to the man then, and hold out my hand for the dates? No, that wouldn't do. He had a stupid, scowling face, not like Mahmud, who is all smiles and brightness. I couldn't expect a man with a face like that to do me a kindness! But I meant to have those dates, and I got them. How? I'll tell you.

I got up, and shuffled leisurely over in the man's direction, as if about to pass him on my way home. But when I got near him (not too close), I clapped my hand to my stomach, let out a howl, flung myself down on my back, and began writhing from side to side, as if I had a very bad pain. The date-seller stopped eating and stared, but he didn't step over to me to ask what was the matter, or to see if he could help me. So that will give you an idea of the kind of man he was.

When I saw him staring at me, I cried out all the louder, and rolled about so violently that I fairly tied my body into knots. 'Oh such a pain, such a *terrible* pain!' I howled, clutching my stomach with both hands. But all the time, as I rolled about in my pretended agony, I kept my eyes on the date-seller; and every twist I gave my poor, pain-racked body brought me nearer to the basket of dates.

I was making such dreadful faces, too, that the date-seller, with the bitten-into loaf in one hand, and the bitten-into meat in the other, was watching me in a kind of stupid daze, almost as if he were mesmerized, and he never noticed that my hind feet were now touching the basket, and that my long toes, which are as useful to me as any man's fingers, were stealthily gathering up the dates.

When I had gathered up as many dates as I could carry, I gave a louder yell than ever, as if I really couldn't stand the pain a moment longer; and stuffing the dates, some into my mouth, and some into my hands, I leaped up and made off as fast as ever I could caper.

I heard a shout behind me, so I dodged down an alleyway, and climbed over a wall into a deserted garden. There I ate my dates in peace. And after that,

I went back to the cabin where I live with Mahmud.

Mahmud had lit the fire, and there was a pot hung above it, and steam was coming from the pot.

'Oh, there you are!' says he. 'Did you get anything?'

'Yes,' says I. 'I found some dates. And I've eaten them.'

'And I found a chicken,' says he, and laughs. 'But I haven't eaten it yet. It's cooking in the pot. Now I'm going out again – maybe I'll find something else. You be a good fellow, and stay here and watch the fire. Mind you don't let it go out, now!'

He went away, and I squatted down in front of the fire.

I was used to minding the fire for Mahmud. For a time I was quite happy, watching the steam rising from the pot, and thinking about how I'd fooled the date-seller, and poking sticks into the fire when it burned low... But what a delicious smell was coming from that pot! I sniffed and sniffed. And then, quite suddenly, my mouth began to water, and I felt hungry again. Dates were all very well; but they didn't really satisfy a fellow's stomach, not as a fellow's stomach would like to be satisfied... And I could do with a little bit of that bird in the pot!

I got up, lifted the lid from the pot, and bent over it to have a really good sniff. Yes, I really believed I was starving! Should I?

No, no! I clapped back the lid in a hurry, sat down again, and poked more sticks into the fire. No, I mustn't, I really *must not* touch that chicken! It was Mahmud's dinner, and Mahmud was my pal. You didn't go filching your pal's dinner, though you didn't mind filching dates from a scowling-faced date-seller. Besides, Mahmud might beat me, and I should have to take my beating, because I should deserve it. If I was good, and waited, I should at any rate get the bones to crunch.

Ah, bones, bones, chicken bones! With my eyes on the pot, I thought of those bones so lovingly that they seemed to be already in my mouth. And all the time that maddening smell from the pot was filling my nostrils...

No harm in just *looking* at the chicken, anyway ...

So I lifted the lid again, and peered into the pot. Was the chicken cooked yet, or wasn't it? Must just see. I picked up a stick and poked it into the pot. And, flick! out came the chicken on the floor.

Yes, it was cooked; in fact it would soon be over-cooked, for as it bounced out of the pot, a little piece of flesh had fallen off it. Better gobble up that little bit of flesh, and leave no tell-tale marks! So I gobbled it up. Then, very quickly, so as not to burn my fingers, I picked up the chicken, and tossed it back into the pot.

I poked some more sticks into the fire, sat back, clasped my tail in one hand, blinked at the steam, and sniffed ... Such a tiny little bit of chicken I had swallowed, but such a big, hungry longing it had left behind it ... Perhaps, if I were to flip the chicken on to the floor again, another little bit of flesh might drop off? So into the pot darted a stick, and flick! out flew the chicken!

Nothing dropped off this time, except a splatter of rich-tasting gravy. I licked the gravy off the floor, and looked at the chicken. It was steaming away there at my feet as if it were *asking* me to eat it. Must put it back quickly, or heaven knows what would happen!

And what did happen, as I picked that chicken up to toss it back into the pot, was that a leg mysteriously came off in my hand.

Well, and was that my fault? If a chicken chose to break itself to pieces in my hand, could I help it? As I joyfully crunched up the chicken leg, I decided that I certainly couldn't help it.

Now you would think I had done enough mischief, and ought to be satisfied. But somehow I couldn't be satisfied. I *had* to see that the chicken wasn't over-cooked. The next time I flicked it out of the pot, it was a wing that mysteriously broke itself off. And the time after that it was the other leg. I was getting reckless now. The more often I flicked that chicken out of the pot, the hungrier I found myself to be, and the bigger the pieces of flesh that happened to break off and find their way into my mouth. Until – oh horror! – there was nothing left bubbling in the pot but the bare back and breast bones!

I tell you, when I saw that, my teeth began to chatter! What was a poor fellow to do now? I had meant to be good, I really had; it was all a mistake! But Mahmud wouldn't understand that, and he would be terribly, terribly angry! He would certainly take a stick and beat me. And though I was as strong as he was, and would tear to pieces anyone who dared to beat me without a cause, I should take my beating from Mahmud, because he never beat me unless I richly deserved it. But I didn't *want* to be beaten! And I didn't *want* my good pal, Mahmud, to be angry with me!

I ran out of the cabin. I thought I would go and hide myself somewhere. No, what was the good of that? I couldn't stay hidden for the rest of my life! Then what *could* I do? If only I could get hold of another chicken! But chickens didn't grow out of the ground, nor did they fly about over my distracted head, like those tiresome kites that had smelt the steam from the pot, and were swooping round, hoping that they, too, might come in for a share of what was going.

If only the kites were chickens, then ...

Suddenly, as I blinked up at those clamouring kites, I had an idea. It seemed to me a wonderful idea, the cleverest I had ever had in my life. And I suppose, if I hadn't been feeling desperate, I should never have thought of it. I hurried back into the cabin, and took the chicken bones out of the pot. Then I came out again, and rolled myself in the dust, till my body was all thickly covered with it. And after that, I plumped myself down on the ground, with my head between my knees, and my behind turned up to the sky, and on my behind I laid the chicken bones. Now I looked for all the world like a big mound of dust, with some bones laid on top of it.

Could the kites resist those bones? No, they couldn't. The silly things swooped down.

In an instant I had seized one of them in my hand and leaped up. It struggled and squawked and kicked, but I wrung its neck, carried it into the cabin, and thrust it into the pot. Then I poked a few more sticks into the fire, and sat down in front of it, feeling well pleased with myself.

By and by Mahmud came back.

'Good,' says he. 'I see you've not let the fire out. Is the chicken cooked? It should be by now.' He sniffed. 'Mighty queer-smelling bird! Was fresh too, I'm sure it was!' He lifted the lid off the pot, peered in, and gave a great roar. 'What's this?' he shouted. 'What's the meaning of it? *Feathers! That's* not my chicken! What have you been up to, you wretched ape?'

I hunched away into a corner. I beat my head on the ground. I moaned and cried. Why had I been so stupid? I, who thought myself so clever! In my hurry I hadn't given a thought to the feathers! Mahmud was dancing with rage. He reached for his stick.

'I'll give you such a beating as you've never had in your life!' he shouted.

I came out of my corner then, and held out my hands to him. I talked and talked, and cried and cried, and told him how sorry I was, and how I would never, never do so bad a thing again. And he looked at me, and dangled the stick in his hand, and made no move to strike me. And by and by he said, 'You're very clever, Bobo!'

'Not nearly clever enough,' I whimpered. 'Only bad, very, very bad!'

At that Mahmud laughed, and threw down the stick. 'Well, so am I bad!' he said. 'I'll tell you a secret, Bobo. The coins you earned for me this morning are still in my pocket. I didn't pay for that chicken, I – well, I picked it up. So I'll just have to go out and *buy* one now. We'll empty this muck away, and we'll say no more about it. Eh, Bobo?'

I hugged him then, and told him he was the best master in the world; and so he was. Together we carried out the pot, and threw the horrid mess away. The kite did smell bad, I have to admit. How could I ever have thought Mahmud would eat it?

So he went and bought another chicken, and we cooked it, and Mahmud gave me a portion of it; not nearly so big a portion as he gave himself, but that was only fair, since I had already eaten one chicken, besides all those dates.

When we were nicely full, we sat together in the sun by the cabin door. And I put my arm round him, and told him the whole story, just how I had been tempted, and how I fell. And he laughed, and wrote it all down in his own language, and here it is for you to read.

13. *The Story of Jacka*

I. THE LITTLE DEMON

Jacka was our crow. When we first saw him he was
only a baby, and he had round, innocent-looking blue
eyes, so we thought he was a jackdaw. That's why we
called him Jacka. He was lying under a tree, and he
was such a mess that you couldn't really tell much
what he was like. He had a great hole in the top of his
head, where some other birds had been pecking him;
and his dull, black feathers were covered with dried
blood. One of his legs was damaged, too; and its claws
were crumpled and useless.

Was he dead? No, he wasn't. When we stooped down, he opened one of those round, blue eyes; and he opened his mouth, too, and made a sound as if he were spitting. So we picked him up and carried him home. We tried him with a drop of water in a spoon, but it just dribbled out of the corners of his poor little beak. We couldn't do anything but make him a soft bed, in a cardboard box padded with grass, and leave him alone for a while. We had a study-hut in the garden, and we put the box in there, where it would be very quiet. And we drew the curtains, so that the light shouldn't disturb him.

We went to look at him once or twice that day, but he wasn't any better. He was breathing, and that was all. Mostly he lay with his eyes shut; but occasionally he would open one of them, and make that spitting sound. It didn't seem as if he liked us very much.

But next morning, the children, who had got up early, came running down the garden from the hut, calling out, 'Jacka's alive! He's up on the edge of the box, calling for food!'

And sure enough he was! He was holding on to that box most determinedly with his one good foot; both his eyes were open, his head was flung back, and his mouth was agape, so that you could see all down his red throat – and wasn't he squawking! We got a raw egg, broke it into a basin, crumbled up some bread in it, and slanted a teaspoonful of the mixture well back into his throat. And he swallowed it, and squawked for more. No, *he* wasn't going to die, not if he knew it! How he ate! He gobbled and gobbled, and when he was so full that he couldn't swallow another crumb, he fell asleep, with his beak wide open, and his feathers puffed out, and his one good foot clinging grimly to the edge of the box.

Oh dear! Had we stuffed him too full? That gaping beak worried us. It looked as if he had fainted, or had very bad pain in his stomach. But it was all right. Very soon he woke up, snapped his beak shut, and called out for some more egg and breadcrumbs.

Later that day, when we thought he was strong enough to handle, we cleaned him up a bit, and washed the dried blood from the wound on his head, and from round his eye, and from his feathers. He took his cleaning up quite calmly, and didn't seem to mind when we ran our fingers over that crumpled leg. Yes, the leg was certainly broken; so, as we weren't quite sure how to handle it, we took him to the vet, who set it, and bound it up in a tiny splint. Jacka took it all in good part; food was what he wanted – food, and food, and *more* food! And as long as he had that, he was content.

He got well astonishingly quickly. The wound in his head healed over, and it wasn't long before he was hopping about the garden with the splint off; though he always had a queer, lurching way of walking, because the bone didn't grow quite straight.

It wasn't long, either, before we realized what a regular little demon we had taken into our home. He was so full of malice, that we decided he must have been thrown out of the nest, and nearly pecked to death, because the other birds couldn't put up with his spiteful ways. He could fly now, and grew into a fine bird, with shining, greeny-black feathers, bright, dark eyes, and a curved black beak. And how that beak did hurt!

You would be strolling in the garden, looking at the flowers, and snuffing up the lovely, breezy, early summer fragrance. Suddenly – a swift flurry of wings, and there was Jacka landed on your head. *Ow!* Before you could shake him off, he had leaned his wicked head over, taken the lobe of your ear in his curved beak, and given it such a vicious peck that the blood ran down your neck. And then, in an instant, he was off and away, up on the roof, well out of reach, puffing out his feathers, and bobbing his neck, and making a triumphant cackling in his throat, that sounded as if he were cracking up coal.

'Got you that time! Ha! ha! Got you that time!'

Another trick he had was to land on your feet, and untie your shoe-laces, and that hurt, too, if you were wearing plimsolls. And if you were barefoot, and there were no laces to untie – look out for your toes! Look out for your book, too, if you were reading! It was Jacka's delight to swoop down and rip the page right across. And, if you were writing, and put down your pen for a moment, Jacka had it, and was away with it up to the roof, where he had a collection of stolen treasures in the gutter.

We had a black Labrador, called Luck. Luck liked to sit in the sun outside the front door, and Jacka liked to hop about near him.

'A very pleasant day!' says Jacka, sharpening his beak on a stone, and giving Luck a quick, sidelong glance out of his bright, dark eyes.

'A very pleasant day,' Luck agrees, with a sigh of content.

'So nice and peaceful,' says Jacka, fussing about on the path in front of Luck, with that curious, lurching gait of his.

'So nice – and peaceful,' agrees Luck, half shutting his eyes.

Jacka frisks a little nearer, pecking about the path in an innocent, absent-minded sort of fashion. He is not taking any particular notice of Luck, no, not he!

But all the same, Luck lifts his head, and opens his eyes with a start. Then he closes them again: his head drops between his outstretched paws; he is asleep! Like lightning Jacka makes a dart at those paws, gives them some vicious jabs between the pads, where the flesh is softest and it hurts most, springs into the air, and is up on the roof, shouting with triumph, as Luck wakes and jumps up with a little shriek of pain.

And whenever Luck had a new ball, Jacka would steal it. He had quite a collection of balls on the roof. He would roll them about in the gutter, and take one in his beak, cock his head sideways and look down at Luck with the most impudent expression.

'Isn't this a nice ball? Would you like it? Well, then, why don't you come up here and get it?'

Poor Luck would walk away, trying to look dignified; and then Jacka would burst out with his triumphant, cracking-up-coal laughter.

'I'm not afraid of you, you silly old dog. Ha! ha! I'm not afraid of *you*!'

But there were just two things that Jacka *was* afraid of, and one was a dangling piece of string. A wide-open window had a great attraction for him; he *had* to fly in and see what mischief he could do. But if you were inside, and wanted to be left in peace, you had only to dangle a length of string from the sash, and Jacka dare not venture. Puffing up all the feathers round his throat, to express his extreme indignation, and keeping well back from the string, as if it were a horrid little snake that might at any moment rear up its head and bite him, he would scold and swear at it. But he never could summon up enough courage to fly past it.

Jacka's other fear was very curious. We had a chestnut cob, called Tom, and Tom liked to come up to the open window, too, and push his head through, and wuffle for sugar or bread. When he did this, Jacka flew on to his back, dug his toes well in, and began pulling out his hair. It hurt, of course, and back went one of Tom's ears, though the other ear was still cocked forward expectantly. That swivelling ear put Jacka in a panic; as soon as it swung back, up he flew with a squawk. The ear pricked forward again, and down flew Jacka, dug his toes well in, and began pulling out hair, but with one eye warily watching those golden ears. The other ear went back – up flew Jacka with a squawk again. It was uncanny, he seemed to think, one ear moving without the other. There must be magic in it, and even a dare-devil crow must beware of magic!

So he never managed to pluck a bare patch on Tom's back, as he was longing to do!

2. JACKA'S TRICKS

One day I was going to post a letter. The letter was in my coat pocket, and Jacka must have seen me put it there, for as I was going along the path to the garden gate, down he swoops, darts his head into my pocket, snatches the letter, and makes off with it. But not up to the roof this time; he had just thought of a new and more amusing way of teasing me!

Between the lawn and the path to the gate, there was a row of small, flowering bushes, and Jacka ran behind one of these bushes with the letter in his beak. I made a dive to try and grab the letter from him. Jacka, half running, and half flying, waltzed round the bush, just out of my reach. And round that bush and round that bush we went!

'Here we go round the mulberry bush, the mulberry bush, the mulberry . . . Ah, ha! Would you?' For I, trying to be clever, had turned quickly and run the other way, thinking to meet him head on. But it wasn't any use! Quick as thought, Jacka gave a flick of his wings, turned, and ran the other way too. And round we went, and round we went, and round we went again!

And when at last Jacka got tired of this mulberry bush game, he shook out his wings, and gave a spring, and sailed up and away, high over the garden, over the gate, over the road, and over the fields, with my letter still in his beak.

By and by he flew back again, and came down to walk about the lawn, and peck unconcernedly at the grass blades. But he hadn't brought my letter back with him; and what became of it, I don't know to this day.

What a little plague he was! In sunny weather, we liked to have our meals out of doors on the grass, just sprawled, picnic fashion, on rug or cushions. That was very pleasant before Jacka came, but with him in attendance these meals became something of a nervous strain. You couldn't keep him off the food, try as you would. George thought he had found a remedy; he would take a few drops of water from his glass, and flick the drops in Jacka's face, and certainly Jacka didn't like that.

Well, one day we were all having lunch on the lawn, the whole family together. It was a lovely day, the sun was hot, and the birds were singing. Luck was stretched out beside us, dignified and mannerly, behaving like the gentleman he was. And, of course, Jacka was there too; but not behaving by any means like a gentleman. Now he made a grab at some fish, now he thrust his beak into the butter, now he flew off with a piece of potato, hid it under a tuft of grass, and came hopping back for more. We were all getting quite furious with him, when George flicked some water in his face.

Jacka gave an indignant squawk, and flew off. And at last there was peace.

Yes, we all agreed, we must be firmer in future.

The next course was pancakes. We were going to be allowed to eat them in peace, we thought, for Jacka was nowhere to be seen. George, feeling pleased with his victory, took a pancake on to his plate, sprinkled it with sugar, squeezed some lemon juice over it, picked up his spoon and fork . . . We others held our breath. George hadn't seen it, but *we* had – a wicked black head poked out from behind his back, thrust itself under his right arm, snatched the whole pancake from his plate, and darted back out of sight again. And the next moment Jacka was away up on the roof, pancake and all!

It was no use being 'firm' with Jacka, he was much too clever.

When, having eaten the pancake at his leisure, he came down on the lawn again, the children fetched out a looking-glass and set it up in front of him.

'Now look and see what a naughty bird you are!' they said.

When Jacka saw the bird in the glass, the feathers on his head and neck stood on end with rage.

'What's that ugly black fellow doing on *my* lawn?' he squawked.

He gave a violent peck at the glass, and that impudent black fellow in there actually mimicked him!

'Come out and fight then!' says Jacka, ruffling up more and more. 'We'll soon see who's cock of this walk!'

But the bird wouldn't come out.

'Coward! Coward!' squawks Jacka.

And he made a quick run round the looking-glass to try and catch the other bird. But the other bird had run away! So then Jacka comes fussing and hopping to the front of the glass once more, and – would you believe it? – there was that impudent fellow glaring at him again, and hopping up and down, and ruffling up *his* feathers, all ready for a fight!

Jacka was fuming with rage: with his head held low, and his wings half spread, and every feather standing on end, he ran round the looking-glass one way, and then he ran round it the other way; but always the other fellow was too quick for him, and managed in some mysterious manner to vanish, just when Jacka thought to catch him by the tail. So, at last, Jacka pulled himself together, and began to think.

'No good getting angry,' he told himself, 'I must be cunning, and catch him by a trick.'

Off he goes, and comes back with his greatest treasure – a box of matches. 'He won't be able to resist these,' thinks Jacka. 'Nobody can resist these!'

Very carefully he opened the box; very carefully he took out match after match, and laid them in a neat row on the ground in front of the looking-glass. Then he stood back, and gave an inviting croak.

'Come on out – you can have one if you like!'

But when he cocked a cunning eye to look at the bird in the glass, I'm bothered if the fellow hadn't got matches also! And he was standing back and cocking his eye at Jacka, as much as to say, 'You see, *I* can play tricks, too!'

Jacka gave up then; he was utterly disgusted. He didn't even stop to pick up his beloved matches. He flew into a tree and sat there, scolding away to himself like an angry old woman.

Though he never actually said any words, Jacka could imitate a lot of sounds. He could chatter in a high voice like a woman, and rumble in a deep voice like a man. In those days there weren't many cars on our country roads, and many of the farmers and their wives used to drive to market in high gigs, drawn by prancing horses. And, as they drove past our garden gate, of course they would be talking. Jacka sat in a tree by the gate, and listened; and, when they had passed by, *he* began to talk. First he was the woman, then he was the man, then he was the woman again. Goodness, how they jabbered! And how they quarrelled, too! For that was what Jacka delighted in most—to make them quarrel. Hearing the angry voices, shrill and deep, that came from the tree-top, you would swear that in a moment that non-existent man and woman would be coming to blows! It sounded so real that we couldn't believe, sometimes, that it was only a cheeky black crow amusing himself.

Jacka could bark like a dog, too. On the opposite side of the road were meadows, with cows grazing in them. Through the day, the cows wandered about from one meadow to the other; but at milking time, Driver, the farm dog, would come down from the farm, which was on a hill above the meadows, and run round them barking, till he got them all into a tidy line. And then he would drive them up to stand in a group at the top gate, waiting for the farmer to open it.

From his tree by the road, Jacka watched all this proceeding with the greatest interest; and very soon he was barking in a voice so like Driver's that you couldn't tell the difference. But that wasn't all. Driver did more than bark, didn't he? And what Driver could do, Jacka thought he could do, also.

So, early one afternoon, quite two hours before milking time, Jacka flies down from his tree, and sails off across the meadows. When he got behind the farthest cow, he came down, and began barking. The cow stopped grazing, lifted her head and began to stroll up the meadows; and Jacka hopped along behind her, with his queer, lop-sided walk, barking all the time. The other cows lifted *their* heads, and listened; and they, too, began to stroll up the meadows. There they all were now, a whole long line of them, moving leisurely up towards the gate, with Jacka hopping and scrambling along behind them, and barking and barking!

Tom, our cob, who was in the meadow grazing with the cows, stood and stared. He could hardly believe his eyes; nor could we, who were watching from the garden. But Jacka went on barking until he got all those cows standing in a huddle at the gate; and then he flew off, chuckling to himself – leaving the poor cows to wait and wait for someone to come and let them out.

The cows had a long time to wait, and I think they must have begun to feel foolish. At any rate, by and by

they went back to their grazing. And when, at the proper milking time, Driver came down from the farm, he had a lot of trouble in rounding up those cows. They had been fooled once, and were not in a mind to be fooled again.

It is perhaps not much wonder that the country people began to be afraid of Jacka. They said he was bewitched, and they tried to keep out of his way. But it didn't do to be afraid of Jacka, it made him all the more wicked. And the very people who tried to keep out of his way were the ones he most enjoyed tormenting. There was an old labourer at the farm who spoke of Jacka as 'Old Scritch', which was his name for the Devil, and it seemed just as if Jacka knew it.

'Oh ho, so I'm Old Scritch, am I? And what does Old Scritch do? He frightens people, doesn't he?'

So he decided to give that old labourer the fright of his life.

It was early morning, and the old man was going up a field to the farm. He was walking slowly, for the field was steep; and happening to look round, what should he see but Jacka, strolling along a few yards behind him. The old man stopped, and picked up a stone. Jacka stopped, and looked at him in innocent surprise. The old man dropped the stone, and walked on; and Jacka followed, keeping always at exactly the same distance behind him. The old man glanced back over his shoulder. Why was that horrid little black thing following him? He didn't like it, he began to hurry— and Jacka also began to hurry. The old man turned and shouted, and waved his arms. Jacka stood still, cocked his head, and watched him out of one bright eye.

The old man was really frightened now. He hurried

faster than ever. And Jacka hurried faster than ever. The old man took another quick glance over his shoulder, and broke into a run. And Jacka broke into a run, half hopping, half flying, never uttering a sound, never letting the distance between them alter by a hair's breadth.

'Oh Lord, oh Lord!' The old man was running for his life now. And still that horrid, black, silent little devil was scurrying after him!

'It ain't no bird at all! It ain't no bird, I tell 'ee!' When the old man reached the farm, he staggered into the kitchen and collapsed. And Jacka flew away with a loud croak, to think up some other mischief.

I'm afraid he had no friends except ourselves, and I think he knew it, too, though he never showed the slightest affection towards any of us. But he liked to be near us. He would come into the house whenever he could; and if you were sitting inside with the window shut, you would look up and see that wicked little head cocked sideways, with one bright eye pressed against the pane, watching everything that was going on inside. At night, he always roosted on the window-sill of one of the bedrooms, choosing whichever window was most sheltered, according to the direction of the wind. Often you would be wakened by a sharp rapping at the pane. We thought at first that Jacka was tapping to be let in; but after a bit, we discovered that he was merely turning his head in his sleep. He was pressed so close up against the window, that every time he moved, his beak would rattle against the glass.

We hoped that one day he would find a mate, and become a little less queer and wicked. But he never did. The only interest he took in other birds was to tease them, and they all disliked and feared him.

One winter, when the ground was frozen hard, the birds came over the garden in flocks – gulls, and rooks, and starlings, looking for food. Now you know that the gull is a big, greedy bird, and not usually afraid of anything; but even the gulls were afraid of Jacka. Over the garden they wheeled and called, but they didn't dare come down; for Jacka was out there on the lawn, strutting to and fro like a sentinel. And what do you think that black imp did? From various places in the garden, where he had hidden them, he brought out stores of food – bacon rinds, and meaty bones, and crusts of bread, and tempting little pieces of fat. And all these dainties he laid out in a straight line right across the lawn.

Imagine the commotion in the air above him: the wheeling and swirling and swooping and flapping of wings, the crying and chattering! But not a bird alighted on the lawn. For there was Jacka, like a malicious old man with his hands tucked behind his back, swaggering lop-sidedly up and down, up and down, along the line of temptingly laid out food, and ever and anon casting a wicked glance up at the flock of birds over his head.

'Hungry, aren't you? But *I'm* not hungry! Look what a lot of food I've got! I've got so much that I can't possibly eat it all! Well then, why don't you come down and get some? What's stopping you? Surely, you great big, stupid things,' (this to the gulls), 'you can't be afraid of little me?'

But they were afraid. And though they complained bitterly, they didn't come near the food.

It was only when we caught Jacka, and carried him, kicking and pecking, and scolding loudly, down to the hut, and locked him in, that the other birds got a chance. Then they came down and hurriedly ate up everything. But when we let Jacka out again, away they all flew.

Jacka had a passion for butter; and, when mealtimes came, he would dart in at the window, alight on the table, cram his beak with butter, and be out again, before anyone could stop him. But one day he tripped up. He was in such a hurry that he mistook the big mustard pot for the butter dish! In he flew, and filled his beak, and out again, before he realized his mistake. But, when he did realize it, what a swearing and a cursing went on outside! We had to laugh, as we watched him spitting out the mustard, and frenziedly wiping his beak on the grass! But it didn't stop him from stealing butter; it only made him a little more wary in future.

3. JACKA BY THE SEA

We had a cottage right down by the sea about ten miles from our home, and for a month or two in summer we usually went to stay there. Some of us went by bus, and some of us drove in the trap, drawn by Tom, with Luck trotting along behind. And up overhead, Jacka would accompany us, flying along the road, or taking short cuts across fields and moors, and now and then dropping down to give us an encouraging *cr-r-awk*, and so flying on again.

Even though he was such a regular nuisance, how could we help being fond of a bird who showed us, in his own queer way, such unshakable devotion? It didn't seem to matter to him where he was, so long as he was with us. He made himself as much at home on the wide, white sands below the cottage, as he did in the garden and fields back in the country.

And he made himself as much feared, too! In the

early morning, when the tide was far out, and the sands were bare and glittering in the sunlight, the gulls used to congregate along the verge of the sea in hundreds, to stand dreamily watching the bright water, and to preen their feathers, and meditate. With the low sunlight gleaming softly on their white plumage, it looked as if the whole curve of the bay was edged with pearls...

And then, with a loud croak, from the window-sill of the cottage where he had been watching them, down on to the sands Jacka would swoop; and, in a moment, all those hundreds of gulls opened their wings and rose and flew away, leaving to Jacka the whole empty expanse of the sands whereon to strut and swagger by himself.

Such a little, lonely, black object on that long stretch of shore, strutting about with his queer, hobbling walk! He looked in our eyes rather pathetic. But Jacka didn't *feel* pathetic, not he! He was the king of all the birds, wasn't he? He was lord of all he surveyed: the terrible lord of whom every other living creature was afraid!

But he did meet just one creature that wasn't afraid of him, and that was a fox: and now it was Jacka's turn to be teased. I saw it happen; and perhaps nobody else has ever seen anything quite like it.

Some half-mile away across the sands there was a high cliff; and, when Jacka was tired of lording it on the sands, he liked to go and perch on the top of this cliff. And there he would stand, bobbing his head, and making his cracking-up-coal noises, and defying the whole world to come and interfere with him.

One day, towards twilight, I was on this cliff, and Jacka was up above me, defying the world from his rocky perch, when, down near the bottom of the cliff, I saw a fox. He was a big fellow, with fat, ruddy cheeks and a handsome great brush, and he was creeping stealthily up a grassy slope towards the rock where Jacka was perching. The wind was blowing from the fox to me, so that though I could smell him, he couldn't smell me, and he had eyes for nothing but Jacka. So I stood very still behind a boulder, and watched.

Jacka, of course, had seen the fox – there wasn't much his sharp eyes missed! – and his noises grew louder and more indignant every moment, as the fox, crouched low, crept up and up that grassy slope and drew nearer and nearer to Jacka. And then, when the two of them were within a yard of each other, Jacka suddenly flew up about a foot or two from his rock, and let out a stream of the most horrible swearing noises I ever heard him utter. He was beside himself with rage and indignation.

The fox stopped, looked at Jacka for a moment with his mouth agrin and his tongue hanging out, and then turned, and began slithering down the slope again on his belly, with all his four legs stretched out, as if he were tobogganing, and thoroughly enjoying it. And every now and then he would turn his head over his shoulder and look back at Jacka, and I could swear he was laughing.

Jacka was now perched on the rock again, croaking exultantly. 'Ha, ha, ha! I drove *that* fellow off pretty smartly!'

But when the fox had tobogganed to the foot of the slope, what did he do but turn round and begin creeping up again, and that made Jacka quite furious! So up and up crept the fox till he was again within a yard of Jacka's perch. And again Jacka flew up, swearing;

and again the fox grinned, and turned and, tobogganed down the slope.

Jacka's croak wasn't quite so triumphant this time. Could it be that the impudent creature in the red fur coat was daring to tease *him*? Yes, indeed, that's just what the fox was doing! And he did it again, and again, and yet again: creeping up, grinning at Jacka, tobogganing down, with his head turned over his shoulder, and his wide-open mouth laughing; whilst Jacka grew every time more flurried and perplexed, and less and less aggressive.

I believe he was on the point of flying away and owning himself beaten, when the fox suddenly became aware that he had an audience. Whether I made a rash movement, or whether the wind shifted a point, I don't know; but the fox, after one swift glance in my direction, made off as fast as he could gallop, and all the fun was over. *Then*, of course, Jacka started cracking-up-coal like anything, trying to cheat himself, I expect, into the belief that it was not I, but *he*, who had driven the fox away.

Jacka's eyesight was extraordinarily keen. From his perch on the cliff, he could distinguish us from other people right across that half-mile of sand. As soon as one of us appeared down on the shore under the cottage, he would come flying – a tiny black speck growing larger and larger until – *croak*! he landed on your head: not to give you any gentle greeting, but to peck you good and hard, and most painfully. He knew he was hurting, and he *wanted* to hurt; it gave him a devilish delight to hear you yell with pain!

We often wondered why we were so foolish as to put up with him! And yet, when on a very stormy night, with the sea raging, and the wind roaring round the cottage, we lost him, we were all sadly grieved. What became of him we never knew. Perhaps he was blown off his window-sill perch and into the sea; or perhaps, if he was blown off, but not into the sea, one of his enemies – of which he had so many both animal and human – found him damaged, and put an end to him.

All we know is that, after that night, we never saw a trace of him; not even one glossy, green-black feather drifting in the wind, to remind us of the wicked little demon we had so strangely loved.

14. *Banks and Morocco*

In the reign of Elizabeth the First, there lived in London a man named Banks, who had a little horse called Morocco. Morocco was a bay, with a long tail, a hog mane, and a flowing forelock. Banks taught him to perform, and showed him in the yard of an inn called *La Belle Sauvage*.

Morocco was very clever at his tricks; he could dance, walk on his hind legs, box with his master, standing up in manly fashion and hitting out right and left with his front feet; he could jump through a hoop, say yes and no, by nodding or shaking his head, find anything you hid, however small, tell you the number of spots on a card or dice by scraping a forefoot so many times on the ground, do sums in the same manner, and point out any particular person in the audience, such as the man who had a green feather in his hat, or the woman who was carrying a basket, or the fattest person, or the thinnest person, or the one who was wearing a blue coat – he could even tell you the number of buttons on the coat!

People crowded into the *Belle Sauvage* yard to see Morocco go through his tricks; he became so famous that verses were written about him, and Shakespeare and other well-known writers made mention of him. Indeed, so wonderful did it seem to the Elizabethan audiences that a mere horse could do such things, that some people even said that Banks must be a sorcerer, and that Morocco must be bewitched. For in those days everyone believed in sorcery and witchcraft.

Of course Morocco wasn't bewitched, neither was Banks a sorcerer; he trained Morocco as you would train your dog, with a lot of patience, a lot of praise, and a lot of rewards, such as carrots and sugar.

But, you might ask, how would that teach a horse to count, or to tell one person from another in the audience? It didn't teach him to count, nor did it teach him to tell one person from another. But what it *did* teach him was to watch his master with all his eyes, and listen with all his ears to the sounds his master made. When Morocco was telling his numbers and doing his sums by scraping the ground with his hoof, Banks would be clicking his finger and thumb together, making such a tiny little sound that no one but Morocco could hear it. As long as the clickings went on, Morocco scraped with his hoof, and when the clickings stopped, Morocco stopped scraping.

Then Banks would bow right and left, and say, 'There you are, ladies and gentlemen, the number is nine! Correct?'

Or, 'There you are, ladies and gentlemen, two and two makes four, and seven makes eleven, and twelve makes twenty-three! Correct?'

And the people would gasp with astonishment, and applaud; and some of them would whisper, 'That animal's no ordinary horse! He's the Devil in the shape of a horse, that's what *he* is!'

Banks carried a wand, too, and the little movements of the wand gave Morocco his clue for some of his other tricks, such as pointing out people, or standing up on his hind legs, or going down on his knees to bow. How simple it all seemed to Banks and Morocco, how mysterious to their audiences!

Well now, after some years, Banks got tired of sticking about in the inn yard; he was something of a gipsy, he could speak several languages, and he loved to wander. So what did he do, but put Morocco on board ship, and take him over to France. He went to Paris, and made a lot of money there, and then he wandered on southward till he came to Orleans.

The French people were even more bewildered by Morocco's clever tricks than the English had been, and they, too, began to whisper to each other that 'the horse was no ordinary horse'. The whisperings grew to loud mutterings, and the loud mutterings to angry threats: Banks was a sorcerer, the horse 'had a devil', no sorcerer could be allowed to live; there was only one thing to do with them:

'Burn the sorcerer and his horse with him!' they cried. 'Tie them to two stakes, make a big fire round them, and burn them to ashes!'

What was Banks to do? Here he was in Orleans, with the whole town crying out against him, and the monks, especially, accusing him of sorcery. He couldn't get away, and it seemed that he and poor, innocent Morocco, must suffer martyrdom.

But Banks wasn't a showman for nothing. He kept his wits about him, and demanded that he should be allowed to meet his accusers face to face, and be given a fair trial. And the monks agreed.

So Banks and Morocco were brought into a large hall, with a clear space left for them in the middle of it. And sitting and standing all round them, were the mayor and the town councillors and officials, and the abbot and the monks, and as many of the townsfolk as could squeeze themselves in. The place was packed, and there was a huge throng gathered outside the hall, too; for there was no room in the hall for all the people who were eagerly waiting to see Banks and Morocco led away to be burned at the stake.

If Banks was in a fright, he didn't show it. And, of course, Morocco didn't know but that this was quite an ordinary day; *he*, at least, was not nervous. So he stood quietly, waiting to be told what to do. Such a handsome little animal, with his glossy, shining coat, his neat little head, his bright eyes, his long tail, and his dainty legs and feet – how could anyone be so cruel as to think of burning *him* alive? But burnt alive he would be, unless Banks could save him.

Banks cleared his throat, and began a little speech: 'Your worship the mayor,' he said, 'your honours the town councillors and officers, my lord abbot and very reverend monks, and you esteemed townsfolk of Orleans, we have been accused, my horse and I, of devilry and witchcraft. But I thank you all that we are not to be condemned without proof. I know, if you will give me your attention, that I can prove to you that we are not devils and sorcerers, but honest and God-fearing creatures, my horse and I.'

'Prove it then, and be quick about it!' somebody shouted.

Banks held up his hand, and spoke loudly and slowly. 'I am *going* to prove it. If I may have your attention, *please*!'

Now whilst Banks was making this little speech, he was turning from one to another in the audience. He was looking for something, and very soon his quick eye found it. In the front of the audience sat a dignified old fellow, wearing a cloak and a high-crowned hat; and fastened on the front of his hat was a crucifix.

'Now Morocco,' says Banks. 'Attention! Look at me!'

Morocco lifted his beautiful head, and his big, intelligent eyes watched his master.

'Can you point out the gentleman in this gathering who is wearing a crucifix in his hat?'

The wand that Banks was swinging so carelessly in his right hand gave the tiniest little upward movement. Morocco nodded his head.

'You can? Then let these good people see you do it.'

The carelessly swinging wand was now making tiny circular movements. Morocco began moving round the ring of breathlessly watching people. When he came to the dignified old fellow wearing the cloak and the high-crowned hat, he stopped, stretched out his nose, and very lightly touched the old fellow's knee.

The watching crowd gasped. How could they know that Banks' left hand, tucked into his belt in such a careless fashion, had clicked finger and thumb together.

'Very good!' says Banks. 'Now Morocco, kneel down before the Holy Cross.'

Obediently Morocco knelt, for the point of the rod was resting on the ground.

'Very good!' said Banks again. He stepped back, flung out his arms and cried in a ringing voice, 'And now, most worthy people, Morocco is going to prove to you all that he is not a devil, but is indeed a most good and Christian horse . . . Rise, Morocco. RISE AND KISS THE CROSS!'

Would Morocco understand? Would he do it? He had kissed his master often; and many a time he had picked out and kissed the prettiest girl in the yard of *La Belle Sauvage*. But he had never kissed a crucifix, and now both their lives depended on it! The clue for 'kiss' was the word itself, and the reward was sugar. But there was no clue for 'crucifix'. What if Morocco were merely to kiss the *man*, instead of the cross? Oh, if Banks could but sprinkle a little sugar on that crucifix! But he dared not move forward, dared make no visible sign!

He could feel the sweat pouring down his back. For what seemed to him an endless time, but was really scarcely the passing of a second, he held the image of the crucifix steadily in his mind, willing with all his might that the image might pass from his mind to Morocco's . . . Ah-h!

Morocco rose, stretched out his glossy neck, bent his head over the man in the high-crowned hat – and mumbled the crucifix with soft lips!

There was a moment's breathless silence in the hall. Then a tremendous roar broke out: they were all on their feet, shouting, clapping, waving hats and hand-kerchiefs, huzza-ing:

'He has kissed the Cross! The horse has kissed the Cross! Long live the good Christian, Banks! Long life to the good Christian horse, Morocco! Now we know that he has not a devil, for no devil dare touch the Cross!'

In the centre of the applauding crowd, Banks and Morocco knelt together. Morocco was feeling very pleased with himself – he loved applause! What kind people, he was thinking. How they like me! And I did do rather well, didn't I? I wonder why I didn't get my sugar?

But Banks was near to fainting. There was a mist before his eyes; he could scarcely see, scarcely hear. He had saved Morocco and himself from a dreadful death. But the strain had been appalling!

As quickly as he could, he got himself and Morocco out of the country. And he never ventured into France again.

15. *Bostock's Lizzie*

I. LIZZIE AND THE CHEMIST

Bostock's African elephant, Lizzie, had colic. Oh, she was bad! They had given her several bottles of brandy but it seemed to have had no effect at all. She got worse and worse.

All the circus folk were gathered about the elephant tent, wondering what was to be done. Bostock had sent for the vet; but the only vet in that small town had gone into the country to visit a sick cow. He wouldn't be back till evening; and by evening it seemed that Lizzie might be dead. In desperation Bostock sent for the chemist.

The chemist was a small, pale man, who had never had anything to do with animals. He didn't know how to doctor dogs and cats, let alone elephants! He came hurrying, and looking scared. By this time Lizzie was on the ground, trumpeting and thrashing her trunk about, her huge grey body heaving in agony. She didn't seem to notice the chemist, or anyone else; all she seemed concerned about, at that moment, was her horrible pain.

'Colic!' thought the perplexed chemist. 'Well, I know how to treat colic in a human being. But this elephant is, let me see, perhaps . . . How much does she weigh?' he asked Bostock.

'Five tons,' said Bostock.

'*Five tons!*' The chemist gasped. About the weight of sixty big men! He began flicking his fingers and doing sums in his head. 'If the dose for a man, in water, is half a tumblerful, the dose for an elephant would be ... Oh dear me, what a dose, what a dose! Dare I do it?'

'She'll die if we don't do something quick,' said Bostock.

The little chemist ran back to his shop, and quickly came again carrying a huge glass jar filled with a murky-coloured liquid. 'It may work,' he said. 'I don't know – but – but will she take it?'

'She'll take it all right,' said Bostock, snatching the glass jar. He knelt down on the straw beside the wailing Lizzie. 'Come, Liz,' he said gently, 'this'll do you good, old girl. Drink it up!'

Lizzie rolled her head round, and flapped her enormous ears. She looked at Bostock with bloodshot eyes, and whimpered. 'Anything, anything, I'll try anything, however nasty!' she was saying.

Would you ever believe that an animal half mad with pain would have so much sense? The little chemist's eyes were nearly popping out of his head as he watched. Bostock held the jar, Lizzie dipped her trunk into it. She sucked up all the horrid medicine, and emptied it into her mouth. Ugh! Beastly stuff! The bitter taste made her screw up her eyes, but she swallowed it, every drop. Then she staggered to her feet, gave another shriek of pain, and looked at the chemist.

'How much?' said Bostock.

'Oh nothing, nothing at all!' said the chemist, nervously backing away out of reach of the suffering Lizzie. 'I'm only too glad. I don't know that it'll cure her. But it may, yes, it may.'

'It's got her on her feet, anyhow,' said Bostock. 'And that's something.'

'But it *can't* have worked already!' gasped the chemist.

'No, but she thinks it's going to cure her,' said Bostock, 'and that's heartened her, you see.'

'I – I didn't know they were as sensible as all that,' said the chemist.

'More sensible than many a human being, believe me,' said Bostock.

The chemist went home pensively. What a lot of strange things there were in the world that he'd never given a thought to! Elephants, for instance! He did hope the elephant wouldn't bear him a grudge for giving her that nasty medicine! He did hope she'd recover! He thought about her so much during the day that he found himself handing a customer wrong change, and doing all sorts of other absent-minded little things that a respectable, tidy-minded chemist shouldn't do.

Lizzie did recover. In the evening, Bostock sent a lad round with a message to tell the chemist that she was much better. And in a day or two, she was her old, good-humoured self again, and seemed to have forgotten all about the colic.

The circus packed up, and moved on. For the next four years they travelled all over England; and everywhere they went, Lizzie met with people who petted her and made much of her. Everywhere children crowded into the elephant tent, holding out their offerings of buns and sweets in front of her searching trunk; and every offering, large or small, from a big bun to the merest currant, Lizzie took from the children's hands with the delicate, finger-like tip of her trunk, and swung, with a smirk of satisfaction, into her great, pink mouth. It was a very pleasant life she led, with everyone so fond of her!

So the four years passed away. And then, in the fifth summer, the circus once more visited the little town where Lizzie had been smitten with colic. Did she remember anything about it? You wouldn't say so to look at her. She was beaming with good nature, and shining with health, as if she'd never had a day's illness in her life. But they say an elephant never forgets. Never is a long word; but certainly Lizzie had a long memory.

When the circus tent had been put up, and everything was in order and ready for the day-show, the animals were taken in procession through the streets of the town. The band marched in front, playing away on their trumpets and drums for all they were worth. Then came the horses, two and two, with gaily-dressed riders on their backs, and coloured plumes nodding on their heads. After the horses came Lizzie, stepping along demurely, her grey, wrinkled hide freshly brushed, and all her toe-nails nicely polished. Then came more horses and ponies, and the bears and lions in their cages, and the clowns capering alongside to make the people laugh. The whole town turned out to see the procession; the pavements were crowded with people, watching, laughing, exclaiming. Lizzie, as usual, came in for a lot of attention. Occasionally her waving trunk caught a carrot or a biscuit, or a piece of toffee, that a child, jigging excitedly on the very edge of the pavement, held out to her. But Lizzie was on her very best behaviour, she mustn't dally and hold up the procession: it didn't need her keeper to remind her of that. She stepped lightly along, and her keeper stepped lightly along beside her, proud of his charge, of her good looks, and her good behaviour, as well he might be . . .

But what now? Suddenly Lizzie stopped, swung round, left the procession, and made a dash for the pavement. The crowds parted right and left before

her; and there, at the door of his shop, stood a pale little man. The chemist!

With a 'yonk' of joy, Lizzie made a bee-line for him. She twined her trunk about his neck and chirruped in his ear, 'Dear, good, *kind* little man! Don't you remember how you saved my life? *I* remember! Never, never shall I forget!'

The procession came to a halt. Mr Bostock hurried to the chemist, who was standing thunderstruck and smiling rather foolishly, his neck still entwined by Lizzie's trunk.

'Don't be frightened, sir, she means it kindly. She hasn't forgotten you, you see!'

'I'm – I'm not frightened,' stuttered the chemist. 'But I hardly know –' He put up a timid hand and fondled Lizzie's trunk. 'It's – it's such a surprise! Do you mean to say that she actually remembers me?'

'Of course she does,' said Bostock. 'And that you cured her, too.'

'But she was in such agony!' said the chemist.

'How could she tell one person from another? And I gave her such a nasty dose! You'd really think she might have hated me for it! But this is' – he patted Lizzie's trunk again – 'most extraordinary! Do you mean to say that she's actually grateful, that – that she feels *fond* of me?'

'Not a doubt of it,' said Bostock. 'Come, Liz, that's enough now, old girl. We've got to get a move on. Say good-bye to your doctor.'

Lizzie didn't want to say good-bye. But she was a good elephant; she did what she was told. Slowly she untwined her trunk from the little chemist's neck, and took her place in the procession once more. But, as the procession moved on again, she turned her head back over her shoulder, and chirruped to her 'doctor' again and again.

That evening, the chemist, having locked up his shop for the night, sat in one of the best seats at the circus. On his knees he had a hamper of fruit – oranges, apples, bananas, yes, and big black grapes, too. He had never been interested in animals; horses, dogs, lions went through their tricks, but he scarcely saw them. He was waiting all the time for Lizzie to come into the ring.

Would she see him? Would she greet him again?

Yes, she did see him, and she did greet him. She warbled to him the moment she got into the ring, the most loving of warbles. 'Ah, there you are, my honey, my love! My dear, kind little doctor!' But she had her work to do, she mustn't hold up the show whatever she might be feeling. One last warble when she had gone through all her tricks, and she was out of the ring again.

The chemist was still holding his hamper of fruit. He

scarcely knew what he had meant to do with it; he had felt much too shy to stand up and offer any of it to Lizzie. But after the show was over, greatly daring, he made his way round to the elephant tent.

'If I might, you know,' he said timidly to Lizzie's keeper, 'just offer her these?'

'I'm sure she'll be delighted,' said the keeper.

She was delighted! She had a grand feast that evening.

And when she had eaten up everything in the hamper, and told the chemist again and again how much she loved him, he said good-bye to her, and went back to his home, a somewhat dazed, but wonderfully happy little man.

'Who would have believed it?' he kept saying to himself. 'Whoever *would* have believed it?'

2. LIZZIE IN THE MENAGERIE

Most elephants are wise, and most elephants are kindly; but of all the elephants one has ever heard of, perhaps Bostock's Lizzie was the kindest. She was an African elephant, and African elephants are not often seen, either in our zoos, or in the circus ring. The elephants you usually see come from India.

You can tell an African elephant from an Indian one by their ears, backs, and foreheads. The African elephant has enormous ears, the Indian moderate sized ones. The African elephant has a domed forehead and a hollowed back. The Indian elephant (just the other way round) has a hollowed forehead and a domed back. There is one other difference also; but you have to look closely at the two animals before you can spot it. If you count an Indian elephant's toenails, you will find there are five on the forefeet, and four on the hind feet. But, on the African elephant's hind feet, you will only find three.

Can you guess, by the way, how many times round an elephant's forefoot goes into its height at the shoulder? No, I'm sure you can't! It seems unbelievable, until you see it proved by measuring with a piece of rope, but the height to the shoulder is exactly twice, and no more than twice, the circumference of one of its forefeet.

Some people will have it that an African elephant is not to be trusted, and cannot be trained. But Bostock's Lizzie knocked that argument on the head for good and all.

Here is another story that Bostock tells about her.

It was winter-time, and Bostock was showing his animals, not in the circus ring, but in a big menagerie. It was before the days of electricity, and the menagerie was lighted by naphtha flares. (Naphtha is a kind of spirit which burns with a very brilliant, white light.)

Under these bright lights a huge crowd had gathered to watch Lizzie go through her tricks; and Lizzie, as usual, was performing with all her heart. One of her tricks was to climb on to a tub, balance herself on one hind foot, and turn slowly round and round. Well, Lizzie climbed on to her tub, and began carefully to rear her body a little, to get three of her feet off the tub. But someone had hung the naphtha lamps a little too low. In rearing, Lizzie's shoulder struck one of these lamps; it broke, and the blazing naphtha poured down on her.

In an instant, the poor animal was a mass of flames. The flames covered her from head to tail, and, maddened with pain, she dropped from the tub and began plunging wildly about the menagerie.

Screaming and shouting, the enormous crowd of

terrified people made a rush for the entrance way. Children were knocked down like ninepins, not by Lizzie, but by the scrambling people. There they lay on the ground, struggling and crying, trying to get up, and being knocked down again. And up and down amongst them plunged Lizzie, her back a sheet of flames! You would have thought that no child who lay in the path of those great plunging feet could ever have survived. But even in her fright and terrible pain, Lizzie had a thought for them.

'She took the utmost care,' Bostock tells us, 'to avoid treading on them. I reckon it the most wonderful sight of my whole career to behold that big, powerful animal straddling gingerly but rapidly over the prostrate forms of the children, as she rushed backwards and forwards, trying to rid herself of the inexplicable inferno which had kindled on her back.'

All this time, Bostock was caught amongst the struggling crowd of people, and trying frantically to get to Lizzie. When at last he did reach her, he managed, with the help of her keeper, to put out the flames. He doesn't tell us how they did it, but probably they smothered the flames with blankets. And then he *does* tell us what gallons and gallons of all kinds of oil they poured over her.

It is very good to know that Lizzie recovered, and lived for many a long year afterwards: loved and admired by everyone who met her, but especially by her devoted owner.

It is an old story now. When, in the fullness of time, Lizzie died in South Wales, Bostock, so he tells us, had her 'beautifully stuffed', and presented her to the Swansea Museum; but unfortunately, during the Second World War, this memento of the gallant Lizzie was destroyed in an air raid.

16. *Harry*

It was a sunshiny day in early summer. A wind from the sea was frolicking among the flowers in the garden, the wide bay was sparkling like a blue jewel, and over our heads the gulls were circling and calling. They came swooping down over the garden like dive-bombers. Hadn't we *really* any more food for them? – No, we hadn't; they had eaten it all. Up they flew again, mewing like discontented cats; and now and then one of them would give a sharp '*Ha! ha! ha!*' of indignation.

We were watching their flight, noticing how long and beautifully they could sail on the wind without a single wing-beat, when suddenly there *was* a tremendous beating of wings, a wild fluttering and commotion. Then, *bump*! Something fell on the gravel drive, and lay still.

It was a herring gull. In his greed he had swooped too near the telephone wires, caught his wings in them, torn himself free, and dropped to the ground like a stone. Now he lay in a shapeless, tumbled heap of snowy-white and pearly-grey feathers.

We picked him up and carried him indoors. He pecked at us all the time, opening his yellow, red-tipped beak in snap after angry snap. But he was too weak to hurt much. His great, grey wings were dangling awkwardly; we stretched them out and felt them; they were certainly not broken, but he seemed to have no power to fold them. We fetched a heap of grass, and made a nest for him. And then we left him quiet for a while.

That was the beginning of our acquaintance with Harry. I can't say it was the beginning of a friendship, because Harry never would make friends. Perhaps he thought we were to blame for his having got tangled up in the telephone wires; at any rate, in all the time he stayed with us, he never took to any of us.

We had had many bird visitors before: there were starlings that tumbled down the chimney, and ate out of our hands; there were redwings, frozen almost stiff in winter, that we had brought indoors, and warmed, and restored to life, and fed until the frost was over, and they could once more dig up worms for themselves; and there was a goldfinch that flew into the kitchen in an autumn gale, and lived with us for months, becoming so tame and affectionate that it was all we could do to persuade him out of doors when spring came round. Even our wicked little demon of a crow, Jacka, was devoted to us in his own peculiar way; though he did plague the life out of us.

But Harry was different. Harry would have none of us. He accepted our hospitality because he was sick, and couldn't fly. But as to having anything more to do with us than he could help – no thank you!

At one end of the sitting-room in our cottage, there was a huge old granite fireplace, about six feet high, and eight feet or so wide, and five deep. We had given up using it, because it belched out smoke, and there was another fireplace at the other end of the room. So we now decided to turn this old fireplace into a hospital ward for Harry. We brought in some big rocks, and some long ribbons of seaweed, and a round tin bath, which we filled with water; and we strewed sand and pebbles on the hearth, to make it as much like a piece of the seashore as possible. And there we put him.

Before the day was out, Harry had recovered sufficiently to gobble up a hearty meal of raw fish, glancing at us from time to time between the gobbles with his yellow, crafty eyes, as much as to say, 'Keep off! I may be hurt, but I can still peck!' He could just stand, but he didn't attempt to walk that day. However, next morning he was strutting around his hospital on his flat, pink feet; and by and by he climbed laboriously on to the smallest of the rocks, and stood there, defying us.

We didn't want him messing up the whole room, so we stretched some wire netting across the front of the fireplace, and he eyed us viciously from behind it. It wasn't very nice being treated like this! *We* couldn't help his having hurt himself, but he seemed to think we could.

In a few days he managed to tidy up his ruffled feathers, and fold his wings; but, once folded, he didn't seem to want to unfold them again, so we thought they must still be hurting him. He was strong on his feet now, and looked very handsome. Mostly he was silent. But we had an old gramophone that the children liked to dance to, and when they put on a record, Harry would bow his head forward, jump from one foot to the other, turn his wide-open beak to the ceiling, and call out '*Wow-ow-ow, wow-ow-ow!*' Though whether he liked the music, or disliked it very much, we couldn't make out.

I can't say he improved the smell of our sitting-room, for we fed him almost entirely on raw fish, which we pestered the fishermen into bringing us every day. Ungrateful bird! How we did put ourselves out for him! Except for not using his wings, he seemed so well and strong now, that, thinking he might feel too cooped up in his hospital, we took away the wire netting, rolled up the rugs, and let him walk about the room. That, of course, meant cleaning up his messes after him; and it didn't improve the polished floor-boards – or our housekeeper's temper! The rest of us did our best to like poor Harry, but she made no effort at all; she detested him – and that was that!

One morning, when she brought in our breakfast, she was almost in tears. She had been talking to the garden boy.

'Dick says you'll have to keep that wretched bird for the rest of his life!' she snuffled.

'Oh no,' we assured her. 'Only till he can fly.'

'But Dick says he never will fly. Dick says he's forgotten how to!'

Of course we said, 'Nonsense!' But was it nonsense? Harry had been with us for some two months now, and, except occasionally to stretch them out and preen them, he never opened his wings. Rather worried, we went to take another look at Harry. We decided that if he had forgotten how to fly, we must make him remember again.

So we took down the wire netting, fetched a large duster, and put on a gramophone record. Then, when Harry began to dance from one foot to the other, we flapped the duster in his face.

'*Wow-ow-ow!*' went Harry, bending his neck forward, and shouting.

Flap, flap, flap, went the duster.

'*Wow-ow-ow!*'

Flap, flap, flap.

'*Wow-ow – !*' Harry lifted his wings, and took a leap off the floor with both feet.

That was better! It proved that he *could* use his wings, if he tried. We did a lot of duster-flapping that morning; and Harry did a lot of opening his wings, and leaping off the floor. But you couldn't call it flying.

For several days it went on like that: we flapping the duster, he opening his wings, and leaping up, and coming down again. But at last, one morning, when he leaped up, he didn't come down at once. He kept his wings beating, and flew half across the room.

He seemed rather astonished at himself when he came to the floor again, and offended with us, too; as if he had made a fool of himself, and it was our doing. He walked away into his hospital, and sat on a rock, and sulked. But he had flown! It meant that the end of his captivity was in sight; and that was all we cared about.

And after that it was easy. We had only to get him out into the room, and flap the duster, and he would fly: not very far, or very strongly at first, but better each day; until he was dashing about under the ceiling so vigorously, that we decided we could now let him free.

So, one morning, when the sun was shining brilliantly, we wrapped him up in a cloth, so that he couldn't make our hands bleed with his fierce pecking, and carried him out into a quiet corner of the garden, far away from the telephone wires.

'There, Harry,' we said, setting him down on the grass, and taking away the cloth. 'Now you are free! Fly away, like a good bird!'

Poor Harry! He turned up his dazzled eyes to the sun. Then he at once cowered down, with his body flat to the ground. He seemed terrified.

'Fly, Harry, fly!' we urged, flapping the cloth. But Harry wouldn't fly. He would only cower, and stare at the sun. There was nothing to do but wrap the cloth round him again, and carry him back to hospital.

Were we going to have to keep him for the rest of his life, then? It seemed absurd! Such a great, strong, healthy fellow as he now was! He wouldn't make friends with us, and yet he wouldn't go! What could we do? Only try him again, we decided. Perhaps tomorrow would be cloudy, and it was the sun that had seemed to frighten him. But tomorrow wasn't cloudy. However, we carried him out, and put him down on the grass once more.

I don't know whether, in the interval, he had been thinking things over, and remembering how pleasant a thing it was to soar and drift with the wind, high up under the shining sky; at any rate, this time, when Harry turned up his eyes to the sun, he didn't cower. He opened his beak, uttered one long triumphant '*Hoh, hoh, hoh!*' spread his wings, and rose high, high into the air.

For a few moments, he circled round and round the cottage; then, as if his mind was now fully made up, he turned and flew with strong, steady wing-beats out over the bay. And, very soon, we couldn't tell

Harry from the rest of the gulls that were rising and falling, drifting and calling, over the sparkling water.

So we went indoors to tidy up the hospital.

17. *Sea Lions*

'Drake, Frobisher, Raleigh, Cabot, Carey! Get a move on, you fellows!'

One after another, the sea lions flumped out of their tank, and wriggled up on to their pedestals. There they sat, with their heads bent back, and their fat, sleek bodies glistening. *Clap, clap!* went their flippers. How they barked, how they clapped their flippers! *Bark, bark, clap, clap!* And *swallow, swallow,* as they swung round their heads to catch the fish that Jerry Baker tossed to them.

'You'll have to do your very best today,' Jerry told them. 'We've a visitor coming.'

'Of course we'll do our best,' their joyful barking assured him. 'We always do!'

The visitor who was coming was Mr Compton, the owner of a big circus. It would mean a lot to Jerry, if Mr Compton would take on his sea lions as an act for his show; for Jerry was all but broke, and to keep five sea lions fed and fit is an expensive business. Jerry was feeling anxious. His sea lions were wonderfully clever; he knew they *could* do their tricks perfectly, he wasn't worried about that. But they were very nervous, and they had whims of their own. If Mr Compton did anything to startle them, or if they took a dislike to him for some reason, they might refuse to perform even one trick.

'And then where shall we be?' thought Jerry. 'On the rocks!'

However, he needn't have worried. Mr Compton was not at all terrifying. When he came into Jerry's tent, he just took a seat on a bench and watched quietly. Drake, Frobisher, Raleigh, Cabot, and Carey scarcely glanced at him. He might have been a wooden dummy sitting there, as far as they were concerned. Beautifully they juggled with their coloured balls; their long, strong, sinuous necks twisted this way and that way, as they tossed up the balls and caught them on their noses, flipped them cleverly from one to the other, keeping them spinning all the time; and, after every trick, applauded themselves long and loud by clapping their flippers together, or slapping them against the sides of their pedestals.

Then Jerry placed a lighted lamp on Drake's nose, and Drake climbed up a step-ladder, proudly balancing it. Nose in air, and lamp erect, he sat on the top of the ladder like an ebony statue. Frobisher, Raleigh, Cabot, and Carey, each sitting on his pedestal, balanced lighted torches on *their* noses. And then, at a word from Jerry, the lamp and torches began to leap and spin. Round and round, and up and down went the spinning lights, tossed into the air and neatly caught again on the sea lions' noses: a dance of lights – a really sensational trick! Jerry was proud of it.

And, after that, came the trick of tricks. Fat Frobisher wambled to the front of the pedestals, where, on a low stand, Jerry had placed a set of organ pipes.

'Time for *God Save the Queen*,' says Jerry.

And Frobisher, flipping along from pipe to pipe, as fast as ever a sea lion *can* flip, and that is not very fast, except in the water, blew a clear, true note from each pipe:

> *God – save – our – grac – i – ous – queen –*
> *Long – live – our – no – ble – queen –*
> *God – save – our – queen – – –*
> *– Send –*

Oh, how he hurried! But it took him a long time to get from the pipe that blew *queen* to the pipe that blew *send*; and a longer time yet to reach the two triumphant notes that blew *Go – od* in the last line. That trick always made people laugh, because when the notes on the scale were close together, they rushed out in a tremendous hurry, and when the notes were far apart, there was a long pause between them, whilst Frobisher scrambled his way along the line of pipes. But he played his piece through without a mistake. And when he *had* played it, he was so pleased with himself that it seemed he would never have done with his flipper-clapping and barking.

Mr Compton was chuckling. 'Yes, I'll take them,' he said. 'Get yourself and your gear moved round by tomorrow morning, and we'll have a rehearsal in the ring.' He glanced at Jerry's shabby reefer jacket and patched trousers. 'We must gay you up a bit,' he said. 'I'll order a uniform for you.'

The uniform was a smart one, of fine green cloth with epaulets of heavy gold braid, gold braid frogs across the jacket, several stripes of gold braid on the cuffs, and a stripe down the outside of each trouser leg. Masses of gold braid! Jerry had never felt so grand in his life! He couldn't bear the idea of even one splash of water falling on such finery. But five dripping sea lions, tumbling excitedly out of their tank, would be certain to splatter him. So he decided to get his pupils into the ring before he changed into his new uniform.

The sea lions were sitting complacently on their pedestals, when, having put on his uniform, glanced admiringly at himself in the glass, and clapped a jaunty green and gold cap on his head, Jerry stepped briskly into the ring.

Heavens, what was this! Drake stared, Frobisher goggled, Raleigh, Cabot, and Carey seemed to be holding their breath. Gold braid, indeed! Epaulets! But this is unheard of! How can you expect us to perform for a jackanapes dressed up in this fashion? Oh dear me, we don't like it at all! Go and take it off!

The coloured balls that Jerry tossed to his offended

sea lions fell to the ground; not an animal deigned so much as to stretch out his nose. Motionless as stuffed creatures they sat and stared. Under his smart uniform Jerry was turning first hot and then cold. They *must* do their tricks: his whole livelihood depended on it!

'Drake!' He took aim and threw a fish to Drake. The fish hit Drake on the nose, and bounced back into the ring. Drake took no notice of it. He was still goggling at the uniform.

'Frobisher! Raleigh! Cabot! Carey!' Jerry threw a fish in turn to each of them. Fish? They weren't interested. Not a movement, not a bark, not a clap from a flipper.

Mr Compton bustled into the ring. 'What's the matter with the animals?' he asked crossly. 'If they won't perform in the ring, they're no use to *me*!'

'It's – it's not the ring, sir,' stammered Jerry.

'Then what is it, in heaven's name?' asked Mr Compton.

'I – I think they don't like my uniform, sir,' said Jerry meekly.

'Rubbish!' said Mr Compton. 'I never heard of such a thing!'

'Will you – allow me to take it off for a minute?' asked Jerry meekly.

'Well, I suppose so,' grumbled Mr Compton.

Jerry darted away.

In five minutes he was back again, dressed in his old reefer jacket and patched trousers. A thunderous flipper-clapping, and a loud chorus of joyous barks greeted him from the pedestals.

'Ah, *now* you've come to your senses!' barked Drake.

'And high time, too!' barked Frobisher.

'Balls please, fish please, rods, and torches!' barked

Raleigh and Cabot and Carey in chorus. 'No more of your nonsense! Let's begin!'

And they went through their performance to perfection.

'It's all very well,' said Mr Compton, when Frobisher had trumpeted out the last loud, exultant note of *God Save the Queen*. 'I like the act, but what am I to do? I must have my show properly dressed. Those rags,' he glanced disrespectfully at Jerry's shabby reefer and threadbare trousers, 'they let the show down.'

'I think it's the gold braid,' said Jerry. 'If I might take that off?'

'Take it *off*?' Mr Compton was indignant.

'All perhaps but a very little bit on the cuffs?' pleaded Jerry. 'To get them used to it. I could add a bit more, gradually.'

'Oh well, if you must, you must, I suppose,' said Mr Compton. 'But mind you, if they act stupid at the show tonight, I'm through – the contract's off.'

So, when his sea lions were once more playing happily in their big tank, Jerry got a pair of scissors and unpicked the braid from his fine new uniform, all but a small piece on one cuff. Then he put on the uniform, and called the sea lions out of their tank.

'Will I do now?' he said to Drake. 'Is this shabby-looking enough to please you?'

Drake glanced at him for a moment. Then he barked, 'Fish please!'

'Fish please!' barked Frobisher and Raleigh and Cabot and Carey, bending their necks from side to side and crowding round Jerry.

The fine green uniform was splashed, and the cuffs were covered with fish scales; the little bit of gold braid hardly showed. Yes, this was their old, damp, familiar-looking Jerry. The sea lions accepted him again, and clapped their approval.

'And what about this?' asked Jerry, thrusting an old yachting cap on his head. 'Will your worships deign to overlook this?'

Yes, they thought they would. They eyed the cap a bit doubtfully at first; but another fish all round had them applauding.

And in the ring that night, before a crowded audience, with Jerry looking just respectable enough to pass Mr Compton's critical eye, their performance went off without a hitch. And so great was the applause and laughter and hand-clapping from the audience, and the flipper-clapping and barking from the sea lions themselves, that Mr Compton congratulated himself on having acquired such a popular act.

In a week, Jerry unwrapped the gold braid from the tissue paper in which he had carefully folded it, and sewed a little bit on to each cuff. In a month he had the cuffs thickly decorated, and added the stripes down the sides of the trousers. In two months he ventured to put on the epaulets; and a week after that, he strode into the ring in the full glory of his gold-bedizened uniform, jaunty green and gold cap and all.

'Now you see, you silly fellows,' he said to the sea lions, 'you might just as well have let me wear it first as last.'

The sea lions ignored this remark. They had rather forgotten what they had objected to about that uniform. But everyone has a right to his whims – they knew that well enough.

ABOUT THE AUTHOR

Ruth Manning-Sanders was born in Swansea where she spent an exceptionally happy childhood reading omnivorously and acting with her sister in plays of their own composition. She was a Shakespearean scholar at Manchester University and, while she was there, married George Manning-Sanders, a Cornish artist. With him she covered the British Isles in a horse-drawn caravan and for two years shared the life of a travelling circus.

She has published thirty novels, two biographies and five books of poetry. Her interests include gardening, anything concerning plants, animals and birds, astronomy, poetry and folk lore.

Heard about the Puffin Club?

... it's a way of finding out more about Puffin books and authors, of winning prizes (in competitions), sharing jokes, a secret code, and perhaps seeing your name in print! When you join you get a copy of our magazine, *Puffin Post*, sent to you four times a year, a badge and a membership book.

For details of subscription and an application form, send a stamped addressed envelope to:

The Puffin Club Dept A
Penguin Books Limited
Bath Road
Harmondsworth
Middlesex UB7 0DA

and if you live in Australia, please write to:

The Australian Puffin Club
Penguin Books Australia Limited
P.O. Box 257
Ringwood
Victoria 3134